Wottaplot!

Wottaplot!

Piece of land vs. peace of mind

Santosh Vishwanath

Srishti
PUBLISHERS & DISTRIBUTORS

Srishti Publishers & Distributors
Registered Office: N-16, C.R. Park
New Delhi – 110 019
Corporate Office: 212A, Peacock Lane
Shahpur Jat, New Delhi – 110 049
editorial@srishtipublishers.com

First published by
Srishti Publishers & Distributors in 2017

10 9 8 7 6 5 4 3 2 1

This is a work of fiction. The characters, places, organisations and events described in this book are either a work of the author's imagination or have been used fictitiously. Any resemblance to people, living or dead, places, events, communities or organisations is purely coincidental.

Printed and bound in India

The story is dedicated to
my father, Vishwanath Setty,
who taught us lessons years ago
that are making sense to me in the present times.

Acknowledgements

I thank all those who had a part to play – directly or indirectly – in helping me shape this story.

I would also like to thank my publisher and the editors who have strived to make my story more beautiful than how I had originally put it.

My name is Raj. Yes, I know it's quite a common name. I might as well say it is an Indian version of Average Joe. Authors nowadays aren't as creative, I tell you. All this guy had to do was search the internet for rare and awesome sounding names; he'd have got a list of hundreds of them. But no, he chooses Raj! If you throw a stone in Bangalore, it might fall on the head of a techie, or on a BPO employee, or on a guy by the name Raj. Imagine my plight, considering I am a BPO employee with this name, the odds of a stone falling on my head are quite even. I'd rather not switch off the author dwelling on this topic for any longer, else he might cut-short my role in this story or even worse, he might make me a second fiddle to some other protagonist.

The Bangalore weather is as cosmopolitan as its people. It was just yesterday that it rained heavily till late night, making it quite a task to leave after office hours, and today, as I travel to office again, being extra cautious, carrying a raincoat and getting a sweater along to avoid the chilly cold in such late night rains, the sun's as bright as an orange.

I listened to the weather forecast just before leaving, in which they said the rains would remain for the whole week. Even after this weather forecast, it was quite stupid of me to come prepared for the rains so much. I clearly don't learn from my mistakes. All I had to do was just ask myself – "How many times in your life have you seen our weather forecast turning out right?" and I could've come in my cotton tights or in a pair of jeans.

You know that feeling when even on a warm day like this, you appreciate the slight breeze making you feel good? Yes, even if you are wearing a jacket. I am at that stage in my life right now. I think this is what they call 'sorted'. Prakhar, my friend, whose name is quite rare and awesome sounding, used this term quite often. Of course, I could not understand a thing of what he meant by that back then, but now that I myself am *sorted*, I can really appreciate what he meant. It all happened six months ago.

I had broken up with my girlfriend Sandhya back then. I have the least intention to make you feel sorry for me, and hence I will keep it short. She was just getting on to me, folks. I mean, she was almost bossing over me when it came to my spending, while otherwise she was quite a nice person. I am just twenty-eight. Okay fine, I will be twenty-nine in a few months. Big deal! She'd always have something to say about me upgrading my gadgets. You need to keep up with the times, which I don't think she understood. And again she kept hinting on more than a few occasions on the fun weekends I would have with my buddies, trying to tell me that I was not saving much. All this was still okay, but six months ago, she kind of took it to a different level when she pestered me to start investing in an apartment. Come on now! So one thing led to another, and guess what? We broke up.

"Good riddance," I told her, as it seemed she was just searching for a reason to break up with me. Personally, I had thought about breaking up with her many times, but then this Prakhar would always try to tell me reasons why I shouldn't do it. Thank god, he's in the US and wasn't around to interrupt this time. He doesn't understand that some things aren't meant to be, and it was kind of reiterated when I told him about this break-up. He strangely didn't react, but said a few words that were worse than a tight slap on my face, "Raj, when you grow old and your grandchildren excitedly ask you about the things that you wish you could change if you could go back in time...," and he didn't complete. He's always been a simple sort of chap, not making too much of a fuss about things. I wasn't sure what had come on to him that he spoke these words. I forgave him that day.

Anyway, we all know when you get introduced to a topic of supposedly some significance, for the next few days you end up seeing the same thing anywhere and everywhere. Yes, something like that happened with me after my break-up. No, I wasn't seeing Sandhya's name and face everywhere. All of a sudden, I started seeing advertisements on plots and villas and apartments and whatnots everywhere. In fact, the very next day at lunch when one of my juniors mentioned that he had invested in some property, it kind of started to bother me. I would be lying if I say I didn't think about Sandhya. I did. But the point is different. She had threatened our relationship on the basis of a materialistic thing. That was not on.

I reached home that day and as I spent time thinking about apartments, I remembered that my father had made me start contributing to some such scheme some years ago. It was regarding a plot of land in the not-so-far Mysore. Back then I had just got promoted to Senior Process Associate in the same BPO. I guess I was quite naïve when my father signed me up. I actually did not remember this during my argument with Sandhya, and thankfully so. But the reason it didn't strike me back then was mainly because it had been at least a couple of years since I had to pay any instalment to that society, and moreover it was my stingy father who had been representing me in this whole thing and I was least bothered. I thought I should talk to my father to understand more about it.

The chat with my father was quite funny back then.

▲

"So Dad, what does Mr Nair have to say about the Mysore plot?" I asked casually. There was silence on the other side, and as usual I assumed my Dad's BSNL network had conked off. "Dad, can you hear me? Hello?"

"Eh...of course Raj, I can."

"Oh okay, so tell me."

"This is shocking. You are showing interest in this, while you hardly even acknowledged it all these years."

"Hmm...things change, I suppose." This was a weird conversation to have. Not sure why my father was making it sound a bigger deal than it actually should've been.

I guess he sensed that as well, "Yes, so as last time I told you, and you lost me in the second sentence when focusing more on the item song on TV..."

"Dad!" Shoot! He knew me too well. But it was Katrina in that song, folks. Of course I would be focusing on her.

"Okay okay, so technically speaking, you have paid most of the instalments, and as per the scheme, they were to get back with the details on when and how much to pay in the last two instalments. I've been following up once every few months. There seems to be no progress."

"Huh...No progress means? It is our money. He needs to show progress. What are his SLAs?"

"What are SLAs?"

"Oh ho Dad! SLAs are Service Level Agreements, which will have details of him delivering this service to us."

"Son, do you think this is your call-centre that they will have SLAs between your company and the client?"

"Dad! It is not a call-centre. It is a BPO." I am tired of correcting my Dad some hundred times on this one. "Your son does not take calls for a living."

"But then, why do you work in shifts? Only so that you can make calls to your US clients, no?"

"Please Dad, that's different. Calling up someone to clarify things as against taking calls for a living are very different."

"Okay, if you say so," said my father, clearly not convinced by my theory. But I didn't get into more details as my focus was on the guy who wasn't working on SLAs; or who'd not even signed any kind of SLAs with us.

"Let's leave that for now please. Now why is this guy taking time? What's he saying?"

"That's the problem. He's saying there are no issues, but at the same time saying nothing on the final steps."

"Can we go to Mysore and meet up with him to sort this out? I think he needs some young blood to intervene, else he'll take you for granted, considering you're very soft-natured"

"Strange."

"What is strange now Dad....?" I dragged.

"That is the exact same thing I have been asking you to do for over a year now, and you never were serious. What happened all of a sudden?"

"Is it? Maybe I never registered you talking about it. Nothing's the matter. I will make time this weekend and we can go on my bike."

"This is a pathetic bike of yours and you ride even more pathetically," shouted my father, whilst on our way to Mysore that weekend. I wanted to give it back that Sandhya never once complained of either. But then he just knew that Sandhya Johansson was a friend, and wasn't aware that we had been in a relationship. Also, my Dad is quite orthodox. He'd anyway have got religion and stuff into consideration if he knew. So good that that chapter was closed.

"Okay Dad, I will ride slowly," I offered. I got that it had been quite some time that he'd sat on a bike, which simply meant that I had hardly been taking him around. I felt a strange prick, but then I brushed it off.

It had been difficult to set up time with Mr Nair for he receives phone calls according to his whims and fancies. It seems he does not receive calls from people whose numbers aren't stored in his cell phone, and he's been constantly avoiding my dad's calls, whose number he did have stored in his cell phone. Stupid guy!

Nevertheless, we had made up our mind to barge into Mysore, like the native elephant would, and ask what our right was. As I'd set expectations with my Dad, I was to do the talking. It turned out to be an easier discussion than I had anticipated.

We entered the office to find a lady seated there; she invited us smilingly and introduced herself as Anu Nair.

"Oh! You are Mr Nair's wife then?" I opined. My Dad stamped my left foot's little one in a hurry, causing much discomfort, which I braved without showing even a flicker of emotion on my face.

"Eh...No sir. It's just a coincidence that we share surnames. Please let me know how I can help you."

Once my Dad shared the registered identification number, there was an animated outburst from her, "Oh Mr Raj Setty and Mr Bharath Setty!"

"Yes, that's correct," and I clarified, "We both are related, and same surnames aren't just a coincidence." And for some random reason, my father felt free enough to give another jolt to my left foot's little one. This time, my leg was perhaps under-prepared for such a ruthless assault, so in a reflex it sent a message to my brain to let the left knee hit the table in front of us with a bang, and I couldn't keep my face expressionless any longer.

Mrs Nair, setting up some ruffled papers, rejoined the conversation. "Hope all's well sir?"

"Yes, top class," I told her, while trying to put the pain off.

"So, this plot of ours," my father began, trying to give her a hint, and she got it.

"Yes, of course sir. Site number 12A right?" she said, which impressed both of us.

"Yes, yes madam. Can you tell us what the next steps are on that one? My son wants to pay off the remainder of the instalments and get done with the registration."

Though I hadn't budgeted a single penny for that purpose, I wore my confidence hat, and just gave a mature nod.

"Yes sir, on that, just yesterday Mr Nair was talking. It is only few people like you who have paid most of the instalments, whereas several others have paid nothing after the booking amount."

"That's bad," came an involuntary response from me. I sensed that my Dad would have tried to stamp my foot for the third time and thanks to all my reflexes I've imbibed by watching cricket on TV, I just pulled my left leg back.

"Yes, isn't it?" Mrs Nair held on to that point, which I got a feeling was something my Dad didn't want her to. She continued, "Imagine how will we be able to pay off all the existing landlords who've helped us with their land to build a good society? We have been sending multiple reminders to people who have not paid anything asking them to expedite. But nobody seems to listen to it. How can we do any development without the money coming in?"

"But then, didn't we highlight the same in the last board meeting, and I thought people agreed to pay once there is concrete information about the registration dates," added my father. Don't fret if you didn't get the statement; I didn't. I just understood that this lady was avoiding the issue and giving lame excuses.

"Yes, that's correct sir. They all said they will pay, but once the meeting was over, none of them was reachable. Tell me what we should do?" she asked. Poor thing, I felt she needed some bit of advice from us. However, my Dad spoke differently.

"But madam, I am already a retired individual. How much more time should I wait to get this land in the name of my son? We wanted to construct a house and move to Mysore at the earliest possible opportunity," saying this, my Dad immediately turned to look at me. Whatever makes him feel that I will blabber unnecessarily? I knew he was bluffing, but I wasn't going to open my mouth and say things like, "Is it Dad? You never told me."

Instead, I just nodded profusely. Then I changed my tone to that of Subject Matter Expert, that I am in our BPO set-up, and talk to my juniors in a certain way to get things done. "Yes Ms Nair. Please understand that my Dad needs to come settle here in around a year's time. I give you maximum six months of time to get all the backend issues sorted. So I hope to see you in the next six months and I will come prepared with the remainder of the amount and we can get the plot registered in my name then and there".

It was clear to me that she didn't necessarily like me addressing her that way. But hey! At times you need to be tough to get things done. Before leaving, I did think of highlighting the point of SLAs to her. But then it seemed as if my father was able to read through me and nudged me to move out of the room. Being under no urge to get my foot stamped for the third time, I just adhered to his request.

"What's with the tough tone and all that?" My father surprised me by posing such a question.

"What else, Dad? They are sitting with our money for more than a few years now. We cannot go on this way," I protested.

"I get it Raj, but you need to understand that she is not the property owner. It is Mr Nair who can do anything about it, and she's just a clerk. There's no use of showing your prowess in front of a lady that way." He surprised me again. But I didn't challenge him. I told you already that my Dad is too soft. People will trample you if you remain that way.

So now it is clear to you why my mood is so upbeat. This weekend is the end of the six months, and I have also managed to save a bit over this period to ensure that the last couple of instalments can be paid and also the registration fees can be taken care of. Whoever told Sandhya that I cannot take care of my investments!

As soon as I reached my seat, my supervisor came rushing to me, "Dude, listen. It seems Preeti is getting engaged this weekend."

I looked at him, and he was almost panting for breath. I always had a feeling that my supervisor had a crush on Preeti. Poor chap never realised she's too pretty for him. I tried to put on a serious expression and patted on his shoulder. His expression changed from that of being in deep shit, to that of being confused.

"It's okay, Ranga," I told him, continuing to pat his shoulder.

"No, it's not okay, you stupid guy," he retorted. Emotions make us do strange things; one of it is being unable to continue having a sane grasp of your tongue.

"Let's go for a cup of coffee," I offered. It really seemed out of place for me. How natural it seems when a guy like Prakhar says this line and people just know that he understands, and get up instantly to move to the cafeteria. It was a difficult one to pull off for me, but I always have been a trier.

"Why are you talking like a fool, Raj? It is no time to go for a cup of coffee."

"Then what do you suggest, Ranga? You want to go to the pantry?" I threw another bait at him, but he clearly is a dumb-ass and didn't pick this up either.

He cleared his worried expression, assessing something. Maybe he was thinking if he could trust me with his secrets. But the next few words clarified that doubt, "Are you drunk, Raj?"

"Me what?" I retorted.

"Okay..." he seemed convinced, only a bit though. "Then why are you behaving in a strange manner?"

"Who, me?" I asked surprised.

"Yes you, Raj. Here, I am telling you that Preeti is getting engaged over the weekend, and you want to go up to the cafeteria for coffee?"

I just shrugged getting a bit confused myself. "What else do you suggest?" I asked Ranga.

"It is month-end, Raj, and your team member is out of office this weekend. How do you suppose you will be done with your vendor reconciliations?"

"Ah! Like that!" It dawned upon me.

"Yes, what else would it be like?" He asked, still wondering what I was thinking.

"No worries, I will get Preeti to work on it and close out before she goes."

"Yes, she's one of your top performers. In case she does not complete before she goes, you will have a tough time."

"No worries chief. I will ask someone to pitch in if she's not able to."

"No no, my friend. It won't be someone; it will be you in case she cannot close before she's out of office."

"No boss, this weekend I am not in town."

"Ha! Trips with your friends over the weekend?" he tried to tease, which didn't come naturally to him.

"No Ranga. It's been a while since I've been on weekend trips. I have to go to Mysore with my father for some personal work."

"Ah ha! Booking some plot, is it?"

"What the hell! How does he know?" I thought, but didn't say it. "How I wish, Ranga. But it's a family thing this weekend, and I am supposed to be there with my father."

"Hmm…good. But listen, it is something you need to manage, okay? The account that Preeti handles is quite critical. I don't trust any of your other team members to do it correctly."

I gave him a slight nod, unable to hide my irritation.

"See Raj," he lowered his voice for some reason. "It is performance management season. I don't want such small matters to come into the discussion with HR and other senior management folks."

This was totally uncalled for. This guy uses this statement for six months in a year to get things done from me. Sadly so, even our performance management period is that long. Before the author goes on to display more of his knowledge on HR practices, let me move on from here to Friday evening.

▲

Murphy's Law just loves me. Here I am sitting with my top-most performer in the team, a day before her engagement, to close out on the month-end activities, and she's making all the mistakes in the world.

"What's up Preeti? You are making basic errors," I highlighted after checking her work for the third time that evening.

"I am sorry, Raj. There are just too many things to finish at home for the engagement. I am unable to concentrate." She seemed to be feeling true guilt.

"Yeah, I was thinking about that. Why would you not plan the day properly? It is your engagement man. But you kept these important things at work pending till the last day. How did you think you will close out on your month-end activities that require focused effort on the last day?" I was both irritated at her as well as sorry.

"I will do it Raj. I will take the spare laptop home and do it tonight or early morning tomorrow," she was almost begging.

"What's wrong with you Preeti? It is your engagement, for god's sake. Just mail me this file and I will do the rest." I gave up.

"Really?" Her eyes popped up.

"Not at all. I expect you to keep working on your laptop when you are with your fiancé and family, trying to celebrate your engagement," I added sarcastically.

"I am so thankful to you, Raj. I am very sorry. I will plan my work better before my wedding date," she said seriously. I was surprised by her pro-activeness and smiled.

I let her leave, and as I sat holding my head and tried to look at the file, my thoughts drifted to an important trend I had observed in my work life. I had joined the firm as a Process Associate, which is the entry level in my company. I used to work several additional hours and I had realised back then that it is we Process Associates who are the backbone of the company. Then after some time, I was promoted to Senior Process Associate. Only then did I realise that it was we SPAs who do justice to our work. Then I got promoted to a Subject Matter Expert, and till now I think it is we SMEs who carry the firm on our strong shoulders. Though my shoulders are quite weak due to lack of exercise and wrong posture in front of the laptop, but do you get what I am saying? I am just worried what will happen if and when I get promoted to a Team Leader. Will I think it is the TLs who really do all the work? But that will happen only when they promote me to the next level, which looks highly unlikely. This author has made me quite average in all aspects.

The HR lady, who talks quite nicely to me, had told me in the last cycle that I am not yet ready to be a TL. It sounded very convincing to me. The cycle before that she'd spent time with me and explained to me how I have a wee bit less experience to be eligible to apply for the next level. It had sounded a bit convincing back then as well. For some reason Sandhya used to hate this HR lady stating that the latter was trying to con me into believing things and thus unnecessarily delaying my promotion. I don't quite agree with Sandhya on that.

With all these chronic thoughts, I saw it was getting very late in the night. I thought of working on this one post our meeting with the Nairs the next day, and wrapped up for the week.

I'd booked a couple of bus tickets, which pleasantly surprised my father. It was obvious that age had made it difficult for him to travel recklessly on my bike.

"So Dad, I have taken my cheque book, my identification proofs, and few passport size photographs. And yes...address proof as well. Hope this will suffice," I told my father.

There was a faint smile from my father.

"What is it Dad?" I asked, with an unsure smile.

"You seem to be ready for registration already. Let's see how the meeting goes. There are a lot of steps before the registration process."

"Oh! Is it? You didn't tell me. Now I have to budget more time then, eh? And why are you worried about today's meeting?"

"They've been avoiding my calls, and also when they speak they don't tell me any details. To expect that all will be solved today is too much of an expectation."

"Dad, you are clearly underestimating your son's ability to convince people to make them do their jobs. You just chill and leave it to me."

"Don't do anything in haste, Raj. We should not cross the line. You won't achieve anything by trying to be outright rude."

I looked deep into my Dad's eyes and asked, "Dad, what have you achieved all your life by being nice to everyone?"

"Listen, this is not *Jab we Met*, and you are not Kareena Kapoor. Let's just take it easy when we meet them today." My father burst the bubble, and what I thought could have been a heart-to-heart conversation between a father and a son, ended up as a spoof of a moment.

But I was not the one to give up, "Tell me Dad, if I remember correctly, you had invested in some plot some fifteen years ago."

I had touched a raw nerve. He gave a long pause and breathed out. "Yes, I had."

"See Dad, I don't want to go into the details on that one, as I know it hurts you. But tell me what good came out of that instance?"

"Well, I got that land in my name after all."

"Please Dad. Both of us know the quality of that land. You ended up buying a plot which more or less is right next to the Vrishabhavathi canal, which carries the Bangalore sewerage. Also the kind of crowd there? Don't you agree that it has a lot of slum dwellers?"

"Hey, but what has that got to do with my nature? It was an informed decision to get that plot of land."

"It's nothing to do with your nature? Dad, you could have put up a fight with the developer for getting you a much better plot, instead of settling for a crappy one. Today, we can neither build a house there nor that plot has any great resale value."

"Listen son, it is a plot in Bangalore. It will surely be of some value."

"Yeah right! Had you bargained for a plot few lanes from there, I would have agreed with you. In fact, then we could have thought about getting our own house constructed. But that is a wasted land. Tell me this, I get that you are not someone who is tough to push back, but didn't you have anyone else telling you otherwise? I mean, the way I have friends like Sandhya and Prakhar, didn't you have anyone who put some sense into the decision?"

My father just shook his head smiling as if I had gotten it all wrong. He cleverly changed the topic, "You have worked yourself up for this tone during the journey. But be careful not to unleash it without there being a necessity on Mr Nair," he ended casually.

▲

This time too, we had come without an invitation as such. They just wouldn't receive my father's call. The watchman told us that Mrs Anu Nair would come in only after half an hour.

Not having got my bike, it didn't make sense to travel anywhere during that break, and let's face it, if we're told it's half an hour, it means at least an hour.

My father, not being someone who can sit peacefully at one place, suggested we go to the nearby hotel to have coffee. I asked him if it would be fine with him to walk around a bit, and he didn't wait to answer. He was already on the way to the hotel.

"What do you want to have?" asked my father.

"A piece of land," I replied. It did cause both of us to laugh for a bit.

I then said, "I will have some tea, Dad".

"Good then, even I will have a cup of tea. We can ask for one-by-two".

"But Dad, you love coffee."

"Yes, of course. Given a choice, I would have coffee. But now that you are having tea, I thought we both can share."

"What are you saying Dad? I will also have coffee then."

"Oh, that's great!" said my father, and ordered for a one-by-two coffee.

"Why don't you order two proper cups?" I asked rhetorically, as I was fixated on two guys having a puff. It was very tempting,

I must say. I used to smoke, though not frequently, in the past. Sandhya had managed to rid me of that habit. But the craving had just begun in this crowd.

"So, you have not been smoking for quite some time?" observed my father, as I gasped. I thought he never knew about my smoking habit.

"Eh..." is all I could gather.

"Oh, so you didn't know I know?"

"No, Dad." I chose my words carefully.

"You seem to be tempted to have a smoke."

"Ahem...Well that's fine, Dad. Not an issue. It's just..." I didn't know how to conclude.

"Hmm...I thought you have left that habit for good. It is your decision. I just don't want to be the reason for you not to get a puff."

I mean this is a 'wow' moment, isn't it? Here I am going slow on that fact, and my Dad is more or less encouraging me to go ahead and smoke.

I got bolder by the moment, and asked my father if it was fine if I took a quick puff, to which he just shrugged and began a conversation with another elderly person, who was a local. I took it as a cue that he was trying to give me some space.

I bought a stick and was about to light it, when I saw a college couple sipping tea and chatting away, oblivious to others' presence. It felt stupid and I felt like an emotional fool for a moment, but it seemed as if I would not be capable of going ahead. I just gave the cigarette I held to another smoker, who thanked me profusely before lighting it, and I went back to my father.

"That was quick," observed my father.

"Yeah, I didn't feel like smoking."

"So will you ever tell me who the girl was?"

"This is eerie Dad. I mean really, come on! First you have known me ogling at item songs when you were talking about the plot of land, then my smoking and now you are talking about a girl, and that too in the past tense. Have you hired a private detective?"

"Ha ha!" He laughed quite animatedly, before continuing, "Experience, it is. That is all. Now let me check if the coffee is done. He seems to be taking some time."

I could also see how he didn't push on the topic of who the girl was. The funny part is that he's known Sandhya for a few years as my friend already. I feel it would be odd to bring her name up.

It's been a good six months since I broke up with her. It was evident that Sandhya was hell-bent on not calling me. I wonder at times if she's moved on easily, or maybe she's got a guy in her life already and has no time to think about her past. It irritates me further that both the thoughts prick me badly.

It was an accident actually; the way we met, I mean. It was the season of celebrations in December a few years ago. The team that I was a part of was playing the game Secret Santa as Christmas was approaching. For those who don't know the game, it's quite simple. A group of people get to choose names of others in the same group, to become the individual's Santa Claus, and gift them secretly till such a day when the whole group again gets together to reveal who was each person's Santa. It seems there are various versions of the same.

These new kids in the team had made quite complicated set of rules and guidelines that could have made even our HR policies take a back-seat. I could have shown that to the HR lady, and baffled her, and on the way could have taken a promotion to the next level. However, I just thought I will play along with my group instead.

The rules ensured that we need to have at least three gifts, and each one had a price limit. I mean, no wonder these are commerce folks in my team.

I had got the name of a new flunky who was the individual to be gifted from me. Looking at his unshaven face and unkempt hair, I did have a strong urge to gift him razors, shaving cream, hair gel and a comb, though it was one gift more than the required count. But I decided not to be mean.

I decided to go to a gift shop close to the office campus. While I had the tough job to make a choice for this lousy guy's gift, a little boy there seemed to be having trouble with his remote controlled car. I presumed it was his grandfather with him, who was really trying but the crowd was thick and the helpers were few. I usually don't butt-in into others' business, but this was not a usual situation.

"Sir, hi. May I?" I offered my help.

The elderly gentleman accepted my help immediately by handing over the car to me. It was a small mistake he had done in placing the battery cells in the reverse order, which I corrected in no time and the child's expression on seeing the car operational was quite priceless.

As I got up to go continue my boring job of searching for gifts, a lady called me. I assumed there was one of my team members in the mall to do the exact thing that I'd come for. But I could not recognise her. "Yes, miss?"

"Hi, this helicopter isn't working properly. Can you help me out?"

"Eh..." I hesitated, contemplating if I should reveal to her that I was not a helper in this store. At the same time, I saw a helper walking towards us, giving me the opportunity to withdraw myself from there. "Sorry miss, you should ask him." I directed her to the helper walking towards us.

"Hmmm...Okay, would you tell me where the train toys' section is?" she asked.

"I am really sorry. I think there's a mistake. This chap should help you, miss."

"New?" she asked authoritatively.

And that authority kind of worked on me for some strange reason, and it was difficult for me to find my words, "Eh…no…I…"

"Clearly need a lot of training I presume." She moved her right brow. The helper joined her, and she got busy with her questions to him.

I was now a bit too irritated and I had wanted to interrupt the conversation and set things right. Only then I registered that it was not just because I was helping the kid earlier that she mistook me to be a helper, but because I had my company's ID tag around my neck, and also I was wearing a dark red shirt that was similar to the colour of the helpers' uniform.

I smiled to myself, and without intending to, looked around to see if there were others who watched my plight. After confirming that hardly anyone was around in the section, I made way to the other side of the store. I found some gift-able items for that team-member of mine and I made my way to the payment counter. Don't ask me what the gifts were, for it is difficult for the author to make up things that can be gifted to a young guy unshaven and hair unkempt, in such short notice.

There was a huge queue, and the inevitable happened there. The lady who had stalked and talked me to embarrassment joined the queue and kept staring at me for some time. I could get this uncomfortable feeling of being watched and I turned to the parallel queue to see she was looking right into my eyes.

It was my turn to raise my right eyebrow. Just that I don't know how these few people manage to raise one of the two brows. I guess I am much unbiased that way and ended up raising both the brows, but she'd got the message before that, and looked away slightly ashamed. I was done with my revenge, or so I thought.

Once I was done with the payment and proceeded towards the gift-wrapping section, I saw she'd followed me there. On seeing her, I tried to formally smile and told her, "Sorry madam, I do not know how to wrap the gift either. You will have to take help from this gentleman here."

"I am so so so sorry sir," she said, with at least a second's gap between each 'so'.

I tried to laugh it off, as we men usually do when a pretty lady apologises. In fact, her saying sorry seemed more embarrassing than the actual event that had taken place not long ago. For back then, there were hardly any people around, but at the gift-wrapping section, people seemed least interested in getting their job done and instead were nudging me to respond to the lady.

"Okay boss, everyone's looking here. I said that's okay. Can we please go our ways now?"

"I just saw you helping the kid and assumed you're a helper. It was an honest mistake, sir, trust me."

"Madam, really, everyone is looking at me now. Let's move on in life to achieve great things for greater goodness." But no. The lady seemed to have taken it upon herself to ensure I turn pink with embarrassment, though that's not even my favourite colour.

As she continued her monologue about how it is true that one must not assume things and get to the bottom of it before forming opinions or something like that, which I am sure I had heard in one of the Moral Science stories, or maybe it was Tenali Rama or Birbal's stories. To come to think of it, Tenali Rama and Birbal's stories seem similar in many ways. I wouldn't be surprised if there are some stories getting repeated under each of their titles. It is surely possible that the South India rights are given to Tenali's stories and Birbal has the rest of India under his banner. Now before she could divulge as to which of the two characters' stories did she get this line from, and before I could move from Tenali and Birbal to other Amar Chitra Katha characters, an elderly gentleman arrived, literally pushing people aside.

I don't know or don't care if he was ex-military, but surely seemed like an old guy who still had a lot of muscle and false sense of righteousness within him and was someone who would wait for such incidents to showcase the same to the others, and perhaps more to himself. "What is going on here?"

"Nothing is going on," I offered, but clearly none wanted to take my offer seriously.

"Sir, this guy..." is all this lady had to say, and this ex-military or ex-black cat turned grey-haired commando held my collar in one hand and his moustache that had several twirls like Bangalore roads twitched a little. I tried to appear all calm, but was almost crapping bricks with this hefty falsely patriotic guy giving dirty stares that don't even suit a valid criminal.

"People like you need to be punched in the face," said this commando guy, and others around echoed his thoughts. I mean, how ridiculous can people be! No wonder this is the sample of our citizens who are willingly and jumpily ready to be misguided by wrong leaders.

I was now almost shivering and things moved in slow motion, pretty much referring to Mr Nolan's *Gargantua*, only reverse this time. It was the situation which had kind of turned up in such a manner that I had subconsciously given up hope and was waiting for a punch to land on my un-pimpled and non-dimpled face, only to become crumpled in a second or two.

How many times, I mean just how many times I tell you that my granny, the maternal one, had insisted on me learning all these chants to impress gods. The Gayatri mantra was surely her favourite, but no! I was one stubborn agnostic idiot who refused to learn any such thing. At least nowadays the in-thing is *Hanuman Chalisa*. How many times have all these random channels that not many watch, give advertisements where you will find movie and TV actors whose face-cuts have disappeared from the face of the earth come to tell us how the powerful mantra of lord Hanuman has changed their lives forever. I, who like an idiot, would watch those channels only for the humour quotient till then, and would immediately move on to item songs, now realised the true value of those chants. Had I paid more attention, I would have been far from where I am today, waiting for the shape of my face to be changed by a self-proclaimed super-hero. He seemed to be from the era of pre-independence to me, quite an antique, you see. At least I will be able to tell my friends that a war legend gave me the mark that rests on my face.

But help came from the unexpected corner.

"Wait!" came a lady's voice and there was pin-drop silence in the crowd.

There emerged from nowhere my saviour. No folks, it was not Sandhya. Sandhya was this girl who put me into this trouble in the first place. There emerged from the confines of a bunch of losers, waiting to jump or punch, an elderly lady who looked more composed than anyone I have ever seen.

"What is happening here?" she asked in the calmest voice possible. She didn't raise her voice, but then I thought who would answer such an old lady, who, though had a very strong presence, might not be able to contain the mad crowd. I was clearly wrong in assessing her, for her question was not for the masses, but for the commando guy. I guessed that it just had to be Mrs Commando.

"My dear, this rascal has been teasing and misbehaving with her," he said.

She looked at the object of suggestion, and looked back at the commando, "Teasing who?"

"Her," he said again and all of us turned to see a bald guy standing there, quite scandalised at the reference from the old man.

"No one teased or misbehaved with me, sir. And I am not 'her', I am 'him'."

Again from this abyss of the useless bunch of folks emerged the main character; the girl with the train toy in her right hand

and the helicopter one in her left. "Please stop beating him up, please stop."

I had to intervene, "Miss, can you please stop suggesting violent ideas to all and sundry? I don't think anyone wanted to beat me up," I said.

"Oh! Thank god. Look, sir..." She was talking to the commando. "He has not done anything at all. I just came to apologise to him for something."

"You mean a lovers' tiff?" asked the bald guy.

"No, it isn't," I said, drawing more negative vibes than anything else.

"Yes, that's right," she said. "He's my friend...I mean, he's my boyfriend. I had made a mistake and hence came to apologise to him. It's just a misunderstanding. Please don't beat him up."

Now Mrs Commando turned to look at Mr Commando, who from a black-cat had turned into a pussy cat. "Honest mistake, one would say," he said casually and tried to march past us.

The crowd, as if they'd gathered for a flash mob dance, dispersed without saying anything.

Mrs Commando tapped at my shoulder gently and said, "I am sorry kid. My husband can get a bit indecisive on certain matters. I see it has not caused any bodily harm, and I hope to presume that it's not caused any severe heartache either."

She indeed seemed to mean each word, and to me, she resembled Professor McGonagall from Harry Potter in her manners.

"That's okay, madam. Just a gap in communication."

"Thank you. And I see that whatever mistake she made, you might want to excuse the poor girl. She made you her boyfriend abruptly only to save you from some good blows."

"Wow, how did you know?" asked both of us.

"It was quite obvious. The crowd, they say, doesn't have a face. But they forget to add, the same crowd also lacks the brain completely," she said and excused herself to go find her husband.

"I am really sorry, sir," said this lady to me again.

"For which of the many reasons, miss?" I asked her, trying to bring a smile on my face, and it spread to hers as well.

"I am Sandhya, Sandhya Johansson. I'd just come to fetch a toy for my nephew while this confusion happened."

This strange accident was what made us acquaintances, and we realised during our conversation while returning from the gift shop that we worked in the same office campus.

I always thought that I am the guy who'd fall for someone at first sight. But this was nowhere close to it. We became cordial friends, and as strange as it may seem, neither of us proposed to the other. Our relation just grew as a strong one without either of us having to put a name to it. I will be honest to say that in the beginning, I was a bit circumspect as we come from different communities. But it didn't matter as we grew closer.

I had not told anyone about my feelings, and wasn't sure how to proceed. It took Prakhar just one meeting with me, Sandhya and her friends, and he confronted me with this. I have no idea how he does it. He made it only easier for me and Sandhya. He was our cupid in the most subtle manner.

It was my Dad who got me out of my reverie, when he landed with the two cups in his hands.

"What fresh aroma, Raj! I was really tempted to buy two cups."

"Then why didn't you Dad?"

"Well, when you can get nearly one-and-a-half cups of coffee for the price of one because of this one-by-two business, why waste additional money sonny?"

"Dear god, Dad! You are unbelievable. How stingy can you get?" Clearly my words were lost on him as he seemed to be enjoying that as a praise.

"It is being clever, son. Making use of available options for maximum profits."

After this friendly little banter, we walked back slowly to Mr Nair's office.

Thankfully, this time around, the office was open. We entered to see a skinny guy seated on the main chair, and Mrs Anu seated at a corner table. She welcomed us with a trained artificial smile and asked us to make ourselves comfortable opposite the skinny guy. It didn't take much to figure out that he was Mr Nair. He was on some call, and we waited for our turn.

The way my Dad used to describe Mr Nair earlier, I had assumed he would be a burly man, much taller than my average height, with maybe a scar on his left cheek. But this guy looked like a geek. So it made me more comfortable as I put my left hand over Dad's chair and his shoulders, and leaned my head to the right. It is a body language thing folks. It is self-invented. Such gestures give you the needed confidence to have such tough conversations. Upper-hand, I say. Yes, you get to have the upper-hand in the conversation. Also, such postures kind of intimidate the opposite party, which was my whole intention. With my position intact, I waited for Mr Nair to conclude his long call.

"Yes, Mr Setty," he said to-the-point, without any greeting or smile on his sly face.

"Hello sir," said my Dad with exaggerated respect, which I don't understand why such fools deserve.

"How come you are in Mysore?"

I wanted to get into the groove and have this conversation, but my father seemed to be answering Mr Nair's questions with great immediacy and didn't let me get in.

"Sir, we had visited your office some six months ago and had requested Mrs Anu that we will try and arrange for any remainder amount to be paid and get the land registered. She'd asked us to come after six months, so here we are."

"Anu, did you ask them to come today?" he asked her, ignoring us.

"No sir. Last time they had said that they would want to get the plot registered, and I had said we will try."

"Ah okay. So Mr Setty, see we are quite far from getting registration done. There are a lot of people who have not even given their initial instalments. The existing landlords, to whom a major part of the land belongs, are quoting a higher price now to release the land. You know, land value has only appreciated in all these years."

"But sir..." my father interrupted, "You mean, we have not even acquired these lands in the society's name yet?"

"That's correct."

"At the last board meeting you had mentioned that only development aspects are pending, sir. You had not highlighted about the land itself not being acquired yet."

"See, it's a combination actually, Mr Setty. There is a part of land where there is only the development part pending, and I had highlighted that in the board meeting, because the bulk of the crowd that day had questions about that. Also as I highlight now, there is a good part of the land yet to be acquired, and the existing land owners are making it difficult."

"But what are the next steps, sir?" asked my father.

"We are negotiating with them for some time now. We will let you know as soon as we hear something."

I thought it's high time I get in, "So Mr Nair, how come we didn't get the portion of land where the issue of acquisition is not a problem?"

"That has been allotted to people who have paid the complete amount to the society for their plots," he answered indifferently.

"But we have been prompt in paying all the instalments on time, sir. In fact, we were waiting for your letter asking us to pay the last two instalments," interjected my father.

"See that's true, but I am talking about people who didn't even ask for the instalment scheme. These people paid the complete amount upfront. So obviously we need to give them some advantage."

"But then Mr Nair, we have been contributing for the past four-five years. Are you saying that if today someone wants to invest in this property freshly, he will be treated on par with us?" I asked.

"Yes, that's correct," he said bluntly.

"Sir, the value of money some four-five years ago was very different from what it is now. How can you say that you will give no advantage to us?" asked my father, though I never expected him to counter this way.

"See Mr Setty, if everyone starts thinking that way, then we will not even be able to proceed with any land acquisition. You need to cooperate."

My father was very pissed off, but I know him well to see that he didn't say anything, for he would have said things unpleasant.

I thought we can at least make the conversation forward looking. "So what are the next steps, sir? If we pay the rest of the instalments, will it help in getting the registration done sooner?"

"That is difficult to say, mister. We are negotiating with these landlords. Once we get to convince them, we will come to you with the revised amounts to be paid."

"Sorry, what? Revised amounts?"

"Of course! How else will we pay for the land acquisition?" said Mr Nair, wondering how we could miss the obvious point.

"So how much will it come to, Mr Nair? I understand you will not have the exact figures, but what's your guess?" I ventured.

"Oh, difficult to say, difficult to say. But I guess it will be slightly higher than the amount you have already deposited with us."

"*What!*" I couldn't help myself from shouting. A few clerks, along with Mrs Anu, looked at me from their desks for a moment, and then got on with their jobs, making it obvious that this kind of discussion was normal in this office.

"Yes, what?" he asked casually.

"Sir, we have paid eight out of ten instalments. You are asking me to pay double the amount again?"

"Slight correction, it will be a bit more than that is my sense. We will update you as and when we hear from the landlords."

"This is insane. We had agreed on the amount per instalment. How can you go back on that?"

"We are not going back on anything, mister. Look at the brochure and all the communication we've been sending. We had highlighted very clearly that the last two instalments will be need basis and we will let the members know about the amounts as and when it is clear to us."

I just looked at my Dad, and could see that Mr Nair was cunningly correct.

"So sir, what's the certainty on when the land will be ready for registration?" asked my father in a resigned tone.

"See, I think by next year same time, we should have some concrete dates for sure," said Nair.

This was definitely not looking good. "In case we want to consider withdrawing from the scheme, how much amount will be paid to us?" asked my father, which I was about to ask anyway.

"How much amount means, Mr Setty? The same amount you have deposited with us will be paid to you. But you need to give us time for that"

"But Mr Nair, even if you consider basic bank interest, the amount would have increased by a big margin. It is an investment we have done for several years now," said my father.

"I understand Mr Setty, but this is not a bank. We used your money to acquire land and ensuring development of the same. We are not getting any interest either. As you are someone whom I have known for several years, I will add some twenty thousand and give it to you."

"Twenty thousand! We have invested lakhs, Mr Nair," I added.

"That is my final offer. Else I suggest you wait for the remaining acquisition to happen, and come back next year to pay the rest of the amount," he said in an ice-cold voice.

I was losing it. "So when will we be able to get our money back in case we wish to withdraw?"

"I cannot promise a date. I will have to wait for someone else to take up your place, and then I will be able to pay. It may take a few months. But my sense is that if I find someone, I can close it within a month."

"But boss, firstly we have put all the money, and then we are not even getting the land at the said price. Now to even return our own money you are not giving us a proper date, and without any interest," I vented.

"Listen kid," his tone had changed and he was looking directly at me for a change. "This is what I can do. If you want to withdraw, then wait for further instructions. But in case you want to create ruckus over this, then I am going to back out from paying the money. You will then have to sue us in the court of law, and both of us know how law and order work in our country. It will be you and your son sitting in my office to collect that amount, if the result turns in your favour, that is," he ended sternly.

My father gently placed a hand on my thigh, indicating me to not speak further. "Leave his comments for now, Mr Nair. So we would like to withdraw. Please let us know the formalities, and we will wait for further instructions from your side. Request you to expedite as soon as possible," said my father with practised diplomacy, which I hadn't inherited from him.

Mr Nair's tone changed immediately to suit my father's, "Sure sure, Mr Setty. As I said, it should be done in a month, and we will keep you posted on the developments." He finished off and we exited the office.

"This is freaking unbelievable Dad! They are basically looting us now."

"Hmm..." my father was thoughtful. "You are right Raj. This isn't going to be easy."

"You should have let me get his collar..." I was enraged.

"Both of us know what that would have led to. It would have been of no use. First of all, our money is held up with him and we aren't sure when we will get that back. With such extreme actions, it would have only become more difficult for us."

"Well, that's true," I agreed after a moment's silence.

"We have basically got ourselves into some deep shit," I couldn't control my language though I was with my father.

"Sorry, I got you into this, Raj."

"Eh...what?"

"I should never have led you to start investing in this project years ago."

"Oh, come on Dad! You did everything with my best interests in mind, and I saw the old brochures. This is his third project, and I gather the other two projects have been launched and people have already constructed houses."

"That is true."

"It is our bad luck, or my bad luck rather. I cannot understand how come I didn't get into the thick of things years ago," I opined, and Sandhya's image came flashing to my mind, which made it further more difficult in my present state of mind.

"It's okay son, all in good time. You might call me falsely optimistic, but I think this guy will return the money."

"Wow, you think so?"

"Of course not in one month and all that. That's not going to happen, but yes, I am confident about it. One thing should be clear between us though. You will not interfere with this guy anymore. He might make things unnecessarily difficult otherwise."

I shook my head slowly, but I knew my father was right.

If you've been tracking, I was supposed to finish the month-end reconciliation the same weekend. Not even a single number was going into my head and it looked like I'd forgotten all my accounting basics. I laughed at the contradiction, for I had taken my junior's case only the day before for making silly mistakes when she was tense about her upcoming engagement. That seemed ages ago, and my soul had gone through important lessons during this one day.

Getting a plot of land in your name was not going to be an easy task.

A few weeks passed since our Nair's debonair talk. I observed myself talking more to my father than I had in the past, though there were no important reasons for the conversations. In fact, I began to visit him more often too.

In our BPO, we are not allowed to carry our cell phones to the floor because of security reasons. Only Team Leaders and above levels have this privilege. Though I am an SME, as I was the acting Team Leader, I had the exception permission to carry my phone on the floor. But you know how it is, when you are authentically not eligible for something, it bothers you every time you make use of it.

It was nearly a month since our visit to Mysore, and my father called me during office hours. I took the call and answered in a low tone which I'm sure bothered my father. "Hello Dad, anything urgent?" I whispered.

However, I didn't understand the reason for him whispering over the phone in response, "No son, please call me when you get out of the loo."

"What? I am not in the loo, Dad."

My team member seemed to have caught the odd word and turned to look at me, to which I smiled and continued to look at my laptop. Thanks to the noise on the floor, my conversation wasn't too audible.

"Then why are you whispering this way?" asked my father.

"Dad, really! I would not take calls in the loo. Now can we not get into such awkward details and you can come to the point please?"

"Yes, of course. So the thing is..."

"And Dad, it is me at the office. You can talk in the normal volume and needn't whisper."

"Ah, that's a good point. Mrs Anu had called."

"Oh!" Now that wasn't expected.

"Yes, I know. I was surprised too, as I hadn't expected her to call back for two or three months. Anyway, she said that they have found another member who's willing to invest in their scheme, and they can help swap us with him."

"I mean wow! This is good, right?"

"Yes, it is. But I feel, by the time the other guy signs himself up and shells out the required money, they might take a few months' time. So we need to be realistic and not expect it to close too soon."

"Of course, Dad. This development in itself wasn't expected. So it is good to know. Let's wait and watch."

"Also listen, Raj. All economic indications show that the land prices may increase further post the elections. So we should also do some homework to see where you can invest this money that you will get, so that we don't waste time once you have the money in your hand."

"Dad, are you sure? We have burnt our hands once. Do you think it makes sense to get into such schemes again?"

"You are partially right, son."

"As in?"

"Let's get this straight. Investment in a plot of land overtakes any other investment option. Be it gold or fixed deposits or shares and mutual funds, the best future return on investment has to be from land and that's final."

"Not really Dad, the other options you spoke of do sound lucrative, don't they? Should I not explore investing in one or few of those?"

"Nope."

"Dad, don't get into assumptions. Let's think logically."

"Son, I have put amounts in all these areas and have burnt my hands already. Need I say more? But yes, it is your money, and I will leave it to you to make the right decision."

"Ah! Then yes, the decision is made. Land it will be. Phew! But let's learn from our mistakes from the Mysore land and apply it in our next attempt."

"Absolutely, son. That's a good point. Exactly what I was thinking. No matter what, we will not get into these instalment schemes. It is going to be a one-time investment and direct registration."

"That sounds really good, but Dad, will I be able to afford full payments that way? I mean, I understand it is a sizable amount that Mr Nair owes us, but surely it is not good enough to fund the complete investment, no?"

"That's true. But we can consider looking into some plots that are quite far from the main city. We may get something at a lower price that you can directly buy from the money you will have. The other option is that in case we find some property of higher value than what you can afford, we will ask for a bank loan."

"Oh, I can get bank loans for this?"

"Yes, certainly. Most of the good developers will have some tie-up with banks. So we can explore that option as well."

"That's wonderful then. Let me ask around if there are some plots available which my colleagues are aware of."

"No no, son. I mean, if you get to hear from some close colleagues about a good property, that's fine. But don't go around advertising in your office."

"I would not do that, Dad."

"And moreover, there are lots of developers who give advertisements for their properties in the newspapers. I will try and shortlist some of them, so that it's easier for us to make the final decision."

My dad was really rocking, I must say.

▲

The coming week when we met, my father already had all the paper cut-outs ready on the table. We looked through them and shortlisted a few. My father also told me that one of his close friend's acquaintances was leading one such effort, and that there were a last few plots of land available for registration. We decided to venture into this one before looking into any other option.

"It is somewhere near Jigani," said my father referring to a place on the outskirts of Bangalore.

"That's okay Dad. With our affordability, we cannot expect a piece of land in the main Bangalore city," I opined.

We wasted no time, and my father took the contact details of the individual leading the project, and the address. We went to see him the same afternoon on my bike.

"I hope you are contemplating buying a car," said my father, as the warm afternoon sun glared at us without mercy.

"Sometime soon Dad. I want to get done with zeroing in on this land thing."

"And you are not getting any younger, Raj."

Of course, I knew where he was going with this. But I appreciate the subtlety in my father's tone. People who I don't know well or I don't care to know either, have come to me with audacity and asked me many times, "When are you calling us for your marriage Raj?"

It's a stupid question, I will call them for my marriage when I get married, assuming I wanted them to come.

Some have been more irritating and nerve-wrecking as well. One of my aged relatives held my hand, and wouldn't let me go till I gave a response to her request, "You are already twenty-nine, Raji? Please get married soon. I hope I will be able to see your marriage in my time."

I mean, really dude! First of all, it was a year ago and she pissed me off by saying I am twenty-nine, when I was at least a year younger. And Raji? Even people whom I consider close to me never call me with such pet names. This lady, whom I see only during someone's marriage or someone's unfortunate funeral is calling me Raji and asking me to get married before her time on this planet. I felt like ending my time on this planet in that instant.

But can you believe it when I say that the above-mentioned incident was not necessarily the most annoying one. It was again one of the old relatives. I don't understand what's with these old people. It must be their endeavour to put everyone through such torture before they bid goodbye, I guess. So it was my cousin Madhumati's marriage where I met the relative. We cousins were doing a lot of running around to ensure everything went smoothly as the bride was a favourite cousin to many. This old lady was from the groom's side. She made me stop in the middle of the hall and explained the complete family tree. After I acted as if I had listened to her monologue, she asked me in a loud voice, "You are not married till now, it seems. Is there some problem with you?"

A good portion of relatives who were anyway discussing useless things now kept mum to look at the senior useless contributor and then to me, and I understood that they had more to talk about now. It was one such situation where you feel like giving some real witty retort back to her, but nothing comes out, if you know what I mean. I just said something about inviting her when I would get married and moved on from there. Now I know why some of the youngsters don't attend these functions. If stupid people enrage them with such stupid and personal questions, why would one go to such functions to get insulted?

Before you get tired of stories related to people wanting me to get married, I just have a last one to share, if you let me. For a change, this one was from an elderly gentleman, who I don't know if I am related to or not, and thankfully, he had no intention of drawing the family tree on the walls of the new house during that house-warming ceremony. However, he claimed during our conversation that he was very close to my immediate family from time immemorial. He also was quite proud of the stock of information he carried about my family. But one last question he asked amidst a few common friends kind of burst that bubble.

He asked, "So Raj, when do we get to see the little Raj, eh?" The rest of the folks laughed at him while he wondered how funny he must have been to make so many people laugh. I think his wife realised that and came to take him away from us, so that he can by-heart all the facts right the next time.

So here, my father, most subtly posed the question compared to anyone in the history of mankind ever has. "Don't know Dad. Still haven't thought about it seriously."

"Hmm...sure. It's surely your choice. But do give it some thought son. Our ancients weren't all wrong in defining yardsticks on life's events."

"Sure Dad. I will think about it," and that was all about the topic.

We reached the spot that was mentioned in the map. There were several projects that were running in parallel was what we could see.

"Uff..." exhaled my tired father, as he looked around.

"Let me get the brochure from the bag, Dad."

"You should have known the details in the brochure by-heart now, Raj," he said in a stern manner, reminding me of my primary school days, when he used to fall back on this tone to discipline me.

"Sorry, but there are so many brochures Dad. Quite confusing," I said.

"Don't worry. I know the brochure like the back of my hand," he said and looked at his hand. "So, where were we?"

"We were trying to find the right location of the project, Dad."

"Yes correct. If I am not wrong, the name of the project is Bhairaveshwara Enclave."

"Oh yes, right Dad. I'd kind of forgotten about it."

"It is right here," he walked towards the main entrance after looking at the advertising board. My eyes were glued to the old watchman, and with all due respect, I had no idea how he was supposed to be the security personnel for this place.

He was busy in his sleep perhaps, and my father didn't care to wake him up either. "Let the old man rest. Open up the map and confirm to me if the plots that are free are the ones in the two hundred series."

I fumbled with the brochure and came to the markings done by my father while he had spoken to his friend's friend on the list of available plots, and yet again he was right.

"Bang on Dad, there are four plots yet to be purchased, and they are from 202 till 205. The rest are blocked."

We walked towards the right place, and I was very pleasantly surprised at the way the development was done. My father acknowledged that as well. There were trees planted, with all required basic amenities in place, and even the electricity poles were all set. It was completely awesome is how I would summarize it.

"Dad, you know what?"

"What son?"

"All that happens is for our own good, 'blessing in disguise' as the elders say."

"What do you mean?"

"The Mysore plot just wasn't meant to be, Dad. Look at this plot. I understand the other one was closer to the city and this one is a bit further, but look at the development, and the nearness to the main road. It is not at all a bad deal for this rate. I should be able to manage with the money that I hope to get from Mr Nair and the savings of the last half a year."

"Well said, Raj. I appreciate your outlook on life. I see you are maturing as an individual. Yes, this is quite a good deal. Now let's look at the available plots. Strange that numbers here say 22 – 25, as against the 202 – 205 in the brochure".

"Let me see." I went around the whole area to confirm if it is the right set of plots we were looking at. It seemed all right, as the total number of plots didn't even exceed 150, and I could not locate any number starting from 200.

"This should be it Dad," I agreed.

"Now let's quickly make a decision. Which one amongst the four available ones do you want to close on?"

"All of them look good to me. Any should be fine."

"Come come now, are you saying you don't have a favourite number?"

"I do have a favourite number, which is seven. But it doesn't make sense here."

"Why don't you look at 22 or well, 202 as it should be read."

"Hmm...I don't know Dad. I don't feel the thing when I read 'Plot # 22, Raj Setty'. You know what I am saying?"

"I know. Here's what I suggest. How does 'Plot # 25 or 205, Raj Setty' sound? And guess what? 2 and 5 put together is 7, your favourite number."

"Wow, that's a good one Dad. I think I shall go with this. What is the next step?"

"Let's telephone that guy and ask him to block it right away. What say?"

"Bingo Dad!"

Dad dialled that guy's number.

"Haan, hello, Mr Kumar? Yes, it's me Setty, Bharath Setty."

Mr Kumar must have said, "Oh Mr Setty. Hope you are at the plot. How do you like it?"

"It is excellent Mr Kumar. I was just telling my son how lucky he is to have this opportunity. We liked the plot very much and want to immediately block the 205, which is mentioned as 25 here." My father winked at me. He usually never does that, but he was so excited, and so was I, for I winked back at my Dad in the same spirit.

Mr Kumar must have replied, "Oh wow! I mean this is the fastest decision-making I have seen amongst all my customers. I am happy to hear this Mr Setty. I will block it right away, and will let you know about the dates of registration."

"Ya ya, absolutely Mr Kumar. The same 25 aka 205. Correct, the same Bhairaveshwara that you had told us about. Hmm...yes... yes yes...Okay understand. Sure, I will call back." My father turned to me.

"I think we should get sweets on our way back Dad. And also thank your friend who introduced you to Mr Kumar." I had a forethought.

"Ah ha!" said my Dad and began walking towards the gate. I like this attitude about my father. He wanted to share his happiness with that old watchman and maybe seek his blessings.

My father reached the watchman and to my surprise, walked past him without waking up the latter. I jogged to catch up with him, and asked "What's up Dad?"

"Yeah Raj, I think we made a mistake."

"Sorry, what do you mean?"

"So we went into Basaveshwara Pinewoods, instead of Bhairaveshwara Enclave it seems."

"That's okay, mistakes happen. Why don't we call up the contact for this pinewoods thing and ask for the details on the plot?"

"Yeah well, there is also a cost differential between the two. So let's try and search for this Bhairaveshwara Enclave."

"No no, Dad. You are not getting it. I completely understand that the one we saw would surely be costlier considering how neatly they have developed. I am okay to invest here, as it seems totally worth it."

"Okay son, you need to get my hints. It is more than double the price of what we came to see."

"So which direction did you say is this Bhairaveshwara Enclave, Dad?"

"It is a bit further," he said and smiled.

After visiting Pinewoods, and landing on earth, we walked a bit further trying to find this enclave. "I think I found it Dad. There, right in that corner, where there is barbed wire fence instead of a solid compound."

We reached the spot and scanned the whole property.

"So Raj, they still need to lay out the roads here."

"Yup."

"And electricity and water line yet to be drawn I presume."

"Yup."

"Looks like they are working on the drainage lines. Should be completed in few months to me."

"Yup."

"Hope you are not comparing this enclave to Pinewoods by any measure," he asked looking straight at me.

"Nope."

"If Pinewoods were a girl, you might have as well asked her hand in marriage?"

"Dad..." I cribbed.

"Haha, it's okay son. If we look at it practically, had we not seen that Pinewoods first, and had come here directly, maybe we would not have felt the pinch, and would have anyway finalised on this one."

"Hmm...I guess so. Let's take a look at the plots," I suggested as we moved to the end of the property to locate the plots.

It was in the middle of the afternoon, and my father seemed to focus a lot on the direction of the sun. Then he looked at the four plots and told me, "Not bad. East facing plots. Blessing in disguise you might say?"

"No Dad," I shook my head vigorously.

"Okay fine sonny boy. I understand that things didn't work out at the Pinewoods. But it does not mean we will stop using the phrase 'blessing in disguise' forever, right?"

"Oh ho Dad, how much of drama you do! I don't have a problem if we keep getting blessings in disguise. But these plots aren't east facing. I think they are west facing."

"See son, this is where my experience and common sense come into play. Do you see the sun? You might have forgotten the school texts, but it rises in the east. And don't you see it is 'Ashtami' today as per our lunar calendar? And where do you see the moon?"

"I don't see the moon anywhere, Dad"

"Rubbish! It is right there opposite the sun, exactly where he must be placed on the eighth day of the lunar calendar. Hence, my theorem is proved," he said with head held high.

I have no clue about the lunar calendar and how the stuff works, and thought Dad was not making sense either. So I would recommend that you need not waste time by trying to refer to some lunar calendar and compare it with what my father just said to prove him wrong. It is surely not worth it.

"Dad, these are west facing plots."

"Explain son. I don't mind a healthy debate, and you know that."

"Dad, it is written on this brochure. Right here...," I showed it to him, where the compass was highlighting the direction in the brochure, and also the east facing plots were colour coded differently with proper legends in place.

"Ah ok!" my father said, and tried to look at the sun again, hoping perhaps that the latter has moved places to justify his assumption. Unfortunately, it wasn't the case.

We stood in front of the plots. My Dad was actually right. If we hadn't gone to Pinewoods and had come here directly, maybe I would not have had the reservations that seemed to be coming to my mind.

"So, do we ask Mr Kumar to block one?" asked my Dad still not looking at me.

"I...I think we can ask for a bit of time, Dad?"

"You make sense Raj. These are not small decisions. Take some days and think over it."

"Sure Dad."

"And will it be 205 again?" my father asked, with a smile creeping up.

"No no Dad. If I decide to go ahead, I will go with 202 this time!" We tried to laugh about it.

It had been a week since we visited the enclave in Jigani, and sipping a cup of tea over the weekend, looking into oblivion, I was trying to decide about it. My calculations told me that even if Mr Nair managed to stick to his promise (if you can call it that), I might still be short of the final amount needed, as I had missed factoring in the registration fees we need to pay to the government. So it meant I needed to go for the loan with a bank any which way.

I got a call from my father right then, "Raj, I wanted to talk to you about this Jigani plot."

"Yeah Dad, exactly what I was thinking about. I think I will go with this. I might have to go for a loan as well for a certain amount."

"No listen..." he cut me short. "I have been trying to contact this Mr Kumar for the last few days to keep him posted. He is not receiving my call at all."

"What's this now? You think he's trying to avoid you?"

"I think, yes. Because I tried to call him from the landline number as well. But I am sure he has the landline number with him and he is not receiving that either."

"I am sure there is some confusion, Dad. No doubt he will not receive my call as well. Maybe he is out of town or something."

"That's why I called you. Can you trying giving him a ring from your number? I am sure he does not have your contact details with him. At least I will feel better in case he does not receive your call as well."

"Fine." I got the number from my father and dialled this number, expecting it won't be received.

But it was received even before the second ring concluded, to my surprise.

"Hi Mr Kumar."

"Yes, who's this?"

"Uh...I was trying to reach you from a couple of days sir. But the number was not going through."

"Is it? I have been in office the whole week. So not sure how I missed it. Tell me now, who is this and what's this regarding?"

"I am Raj, sir"

"Sorry, who Raj?"

"Sir, I am Bharath Setty's son. My Dad has been trying to reach you since a couple of days."

There was an uncomfortable silence from the other end, making it obvious to me that my father was right in understanding this Mr Kumar.

"Ah, yes. I have been busy in office work. So I could not answer your father's call. I will call him back when I can. Anything else?"

"I think now that I have called you, I will anyway convey my decision to you on that piece of land."

"Oh sure, tell me please. Which one are you freezing on? And when do you want to come down to get the papers for registration?"

"Sir, I want you to block site number 202. I will pay the booking amount to you next week, and then we will do bulk payment once we get some money that we are expecting next month."

"See Raj! We cannot wait for so long. These are hot-selling properties. Out of the four available ones, 202 and 205 have already been booked, and next week is the registration for those. So you tell me if you can arrange for the complete amount in a week's time, and we can think of blocking one of the two available plots." He sounded too matter-of-fact.

"Sir, arranging everything in a week's time..."

"I had told your father when I spoke to him last time as well. We are having multiple people waiting to book the plots. If you want to wait for long or go for a bank loan, then I suggest you wait for our next project. Call me back by tomorrow if you will be able to arrange for the amount in a week's time. Thank you."

I called up my father again, "Dad, what had you told him the last time you spoke to him?"

"Nothing in particular. I had called up and asked him for time for a few days to make a decision. It was the same evening after we were done visiting the plot."

"Not that Dad. Had you told him anything about the mode of pay-out or any other details related to that?"

"Oh that? Yes. I told him that we don't have any ready cash, and we need time to arrange for it."

"No wonder!"

"What?"

"He'd been intentionally avoiding you Dad. These people are looking for folks who can pay immediate cash and get the registration done."

"That is so unfair. Does he expect all of us to be cash rich?"

"I don't know that, Dad. But it was quite obvious when I spoke to him just now."

"Such an unethical set of people. I mean, if we had raw cash to use, then we'd rather have gone to Pinewoods instead of trying to make a deal with this stupid guy."

"Exactly Dad!"

"So what did he say? I mean, how did the conversation end?"

"Dad, there are many willing to buy a plot. He will find people in quick time who would want to pay the whole amount in one shot and get it. He won't waste his time with us anymore."

"I understand most people do that. But this Kumar was a good acquaintance of a close friend. At least they should have basic courtesy."

I was already quite frustrated, but I could sense the disappointment in my Dad's voice, and hence didn't say anything. It kind of touched a nerve, when he was trying to console me, "Don't get worked up Raj. We will get a good plot for you. We will try and find other options. Don't feel disappointed."

"Sure Dad, why should I be worried when I have you with me."

We ended the conversation by agreeing to go visit other places whose advertisements we had seen in the papers. My father also added that I should keep my eyes and ears open in this matter, just in case I got to know about any red hot deal that I could get myself into.

▲

I observed that I had become less of a workaholic of late. It was as if I had got a direction in my life sort of a feeling. In the cafeteria the coming week, exactly the same thing happened that my father had asked me to anticipate. The news had travelled to our table that someone from the neighbouring team had just bought a plot the preceding week, and dirt cheap. On trying to appear as casual as possible and enquiring, I got to know it was one of the SMEs, and thankfully someone who I was in talking terms with, as he too was a tenured employee. That's why we need to be good to others, and learn to at least greet each other the way I did with this guy. You never know whose help you might need at times.

"Hey Pramod," I had validated his full name with my junior at the lunch table before approaching him.

"What's up, hero?" he said and smiled broadly. He may have been putting up a fake one, but looked very natural and genuine, as if he was happy to see me. That is completely fine folks. I don't expect him to know my name. I didn't either, right? This nevertheless reminded me of my first boss, who would call any of his team members 'Champ', for it was obvious that he never registered any of our names, though somehow he would remember names of all the ladies in the department.

"Got a minute, Pramod?"

"I am busy, yes. But for people like you Raj, I can surely make time."

Woah! I didn't see this coming. He knew my name and he was saying that he could make time for me. I tried to quickly recollect just in case if I had done any favour to him that I was forgetting at the moment. Well, I don't go around doing favours, but I just thought I should sweep my brain quickly once, but I found no such fortunate event.

"Tell me sir," he asked me when we went to the pantry.

"Sorry to bother man. I will make it quick. And I don't like interfering in your personal stuff, but I heard you got a plot or something."

"Yes, that's correct. Tell me what you want to know."

"Any headway you can give will help, Pramod. I just have been trying to explore options. Nothing has worked out, so when I heard about you, I thought it is better I check with you directly."

"Hey no problem, Raj. Happy to help you man. I will email you the contact information of the developer. And listen, I have been told by the developer that if I introduce anyone, I will get a small token from him."

"No worries at all man. I will ensure I give your details as reference when I speak to him."

"No Raj, I couldn't do that with you."

"Excuse me?" I blurted out before I could stop myself.

"You really think I will take commission from a deal that involves you? I just wanted to tell you that you look at the property once and if you plan to finalise, just let me know. I will talk to the developer and ask him to reduce the amount which he otherwise would have given to me from your payment."

"Are you kidding me?!" I told myself. Maybe I was just too loud in my head or perhaps he could read my expression.

"What Raj? You seem a bit taken aback with what I said."

"Eh...well of course Pramod. I am unable to understand why you would give up something. That too for someone like me." I just could not mince words and said it as directly as I could.

"It will go to hell if I take money from people like you man."

"What the hell? I mean, what hell are you referring to? I am sorry, I am lost."

"Come on Raj. You are one of the nicest guys around, and I have a lot to learn from you. It will be an insult to me to take any money from you. My girlfriend just loves you."

"Excuse me?" Yes, I continued to use the same tone for I was more lost now. Why would his girlfriend love me?? Even my own girlfriend stopped loving me.

"Dude, I remember six months ago you had your break-up. I mean, all the tenured ones know about you and what's her name... Sandhya right? You both used to catch up in the common coffee shop in the campus quite often."

"Oh!"

Now this guy and his girlfriend are stalking me or what? For the moment, I felt that I didn't need the details of the plot from him.

"Sorry, I see I am embarrassing you."

"Well, kind of."

"I will make it short. What I mean is, it was obvious when you and Sandhya broke up, for I stopped seeing you both when I would go down for a smoke often. It was more pronounced when you were so hurt from the whole episode that you fell sick for a few days, and didn't turn up in office. I mentioned it in a casual conversation to my girlfriend, and man she's become a fan of you."

"Oh that! No no no Pramod, it is not what you think it is, buddy."

"Ha...humility, is it?"

"No dude, it is not the case."

"Okay sure, then tell me what the case is?" He asked promptly, as I searched for words and could not say anything.

"I also know that you still don't have a girlfriend, and my girlfriend thinks you are still in love with Sandhya."

"Okay Pramod, you are freaking me out man."

"No no, let's not get into more details. I understand it's your personal stuff, and I will not talk anymore on that. But yes, you are my hero, our hero," he said with a lot of thrust and trust in his voice, but looked to me like the old Boost advertisement with Kapil and Sachin in it.

He continued, "I will email you all the details you need, and please don't forget to inform me in case you want to finalise this. My girlfriend will end up breaking up with me if I take money from you," he concluded and left for his workstation, giving me some relief.

Folks, don't go by what he said, for it is a lie. Yes, I agree that I fell sick for a few days in the following week after breaking up with Sandhya, but it was not because of her that I fell ill. Don't get me wrong, I am not saying that I didn't feel bad. Between us, I confess that I felt rather miserable. But that's that. End of the story.

Okay fine, you will get it out of me, I see. In fact, I choose to let you know, else you will become a member of 'Pramod, girlfriend and co.' and have false notions about me, which I cannot afford to let happen.

After a week or so since I'd stopped speaking to Sandhya, there was this uneasiness that had crept in. Of late, I was getting quite irritable about small things and a couple of times it happened with my colleagues as well. As a person, I had always taken pride in keeping my personal and professional lives separate and ensured either should not affect the other in a bad way. But now I knew I had crossed that line, which further increased my frustration, making it a vicious circle, which if continued, might have pulled me down into a negative spiral. No, I would not let something like that happen.

Upcoming was a public holiday on a Friday, and I made a quick decision to spend time outside Bangalore. I thought of my family and friends whom I could team up with for a small vacation over the long weekend, but held on to my current thoughts as a new and a unique one emerged. If I were a cartoon, which let me assure you I am not, then it was quite possible that one would have seen a small bulb go off near my head indicating that I'd got a fantastic idea. I decided to go on a vacation all alone! Yes, this was not something I had done before, but as if the universe conspired, few of my friends' experiences that they had shared several months ago on the 'me' time they found during such vacations and how energised and sorted they felt after such vacations, just came to me in a flash.

With that plan, I began to search all the travel websites and it wasn't encouraging to find that most of the good places, including small homestays, were already blocked. I hurled few curses at others in Bangalore, who probably live only for long weekends and ensure they block off all possible avenues of vacation when such a weekend arrives. A thought did cross my mind if it made sense to just stay back in Bangalore considering half of the city would anyway be empty during long weekends, and I could still end up spending time alone that way, without any unnecessary disturbance during the vacation, as it would otherwise have been. But that didn't sound promising. I had to go out of Bangalore alone for me to recuperate is the answer that my soul gave me.

Again, the universe, within a span of minutes, conspired to show me some lodge in Bandipur, when I hit a key on the laptop accidentally. It had reasonable comments from some travellers as well. The thought of thick vegetation, coupled by mountainous regions, and the possibility of spending time with wildlife just added up in my mind better than a balance sheet would. Without thinking twice, I blocked two nights in that lodge, and waited expectantly for the weekend to arrive. I had told myself that I was a human being. No, I was a human being even otherwise. I meant that as I was a mere human being, it is possible that I might continue to get irritated with minor stuff till the weekend arrived. So I had told myself that in such instances, all I had to do was close my eyes, take a deep breath, think of greenery, mist covered mountains, tranquillity and the chirping of birds that I would be experiencing in Bandipur, and that would lead to me calming down.

At last, the weekend arrived. I began my journey on my bike early in the morning and travelled for a long time in the warm day prepared to rejuvenate in Bandipur Tiger Reserve area. While travelling, I double checked whether I had packed all the required stuff that would be needed when I reached there. There was a time when I had travelled to a hilly region in Tamil Nadu on vacation with some of my friends, where I had not taken any woollen clothes.

I was frozen like an ice cream and had to make an exception request for a room heater. When all my friends enjoyed the beautiful surroundings quite well, I had become infamous for sitting in front of the heater all day long, more so at nights, and finishing reading three books by Agatha Christie. While I had found those books quite interesting, my friends had teased me for weeks to come on how I had ruined my holiday by coming ill prepared.

Such ill preparation was not going to bother me this time, I knew. I had ensured that I prepared a checklist and had gathered all the items needed for me to get to Bandipur. This time, I had ensured I had gotten more woollen clothes to guarantee I didn't have to worry about room heaters and stuff.

It was a bit thrilling to pass through the forest as I neared the lodge after having travelled for around five hours, and stopped a couple of times when I spotted deer and once more when I heard a peacock. I was already beginning to feel good about the whole thing.

With some directions on GPS, I managed to reach the lodge at the expected time. At the reception, a few people, and also the owner of the property, a certain gentleman called Mr Alex, joined in to welcome me.

I couldn't hide my curiosity anymore. "How come I see so many of you waiting to welcome me?" I asked Mr. Alex.

"It is a pleasure welcoming guests like you, sir. It is not the peak season here, and it is because of people like you that we get business in such off-season." He couldn't hide his excitement.

"Oh! It is off-season?"

"Yes, sir. It is quite hot and dry during this season and we rarely have guests, as you can see."

It was then that it hit me that in the middle of all the deer watching and listening to peacock, I hadn't registered that it was hot as a furnace, unlike how I had envisaged it. Also, it then made sense to me that there were no other guests in the lodge, which is one of the reasons why so many members of the staff had *gheraoed* me in the name of welcoming, as they had none else to serve.

It was a let-down for me, but then I made up my mind that no matter what, I would still have a great time in the couple of days I had decided to spend there.

"Which room do you prefer, sir?" asked the receptionist. This was something cool, as I pretty much had all of the property from which I could choose.

"Which one do you suggest, sir?" I put the question back. It always works. Anyone asks me questions at office I have no clue about, I just question them back, and it gets solved. Confidence and body language are key, I would say.

"Sir, I think there is this suite..."

"I suggest you give the forest facing room to Mr Raj." It was Mr Alex speaking from a distance.

"Oh sure, sir. That is a great idea," said the receptionist.

"Why, what's good about that room?" I inquired.

"Sir, that is a wonderful room with a hundred and eighty degree view of the forest. There have been several instances where animals have been spotted by our guests. In fact Mr Raj, there have been instances where my guests have vacated the premises because that room was not free to be allotted to them."

The rest of his employees nodded, and I said, "So the forest facing room it is then."

Though I had limited luggage, the helper insisted on carrying it, and I let him. On the way, he said, "Sir, have you got a good camera?"

I hadn't and told him so. I just thought this should get into the list of items I had prepared as the checklist for the next time.

"Sir, there was this foreign guest who visited last month, and spent time sitting in the open veranda till two in the morning, with a special camera and captured some wonderful shots, sir. He refused to transfer the photos to us and said that those are for professional work. Maybe there is demand for such photos."

"So then you do have good animal traffic here in the jungle?" I questioned.

"Yes sir. I guarantee you will see some or the other animal on a frequent basis from this room."

"Some wild animals like tiger or leopards spotted here?"

"No, sir. Tiger, I had seen only once when I had taken people for a safari. It was nearly two years ago. But yes, I have seen a leopard many times." He seemed to be an honest chap.

"What's your name?"

"I am Mahesha, sir"

"Hmm...Mahesh..."

"No sir, it is Mahesha."

"Alright Mahesha," I smiled and tipped him. He refused to collect it and said that at the end of the stay, if I feel like, I could drop the tip amount in a drop box that they'd left in the reception area.

I freshened up, and though I felt sleepy, I thought I would spend some time sitting in the open veranda and have a cup of tea. As the evening swept over, the cool breeze made me overcome the initial disappointment I'd had about the weather. Moreover, in a matter of an hour, I had seen few many deer and a pair of hare lurking around carefree that made the evening enjoyable. There was a thin electric fence that separated my room and the jungle.

I decided to have a quick dinner and get back to bed to rest my tired body. I thought I would get completely drunk, and then wake up as a new person in the morning. So I went to the receptionist to check, "What do you have for drinks?"

He relayed that question to the restaurant, and a helper emerged to announce, "Black tea, milk tea, ginger tea, masala tea, black coffee, milk coffee, lime juice..."

"Wait, my friend. I wanted to ask about liquor."

"Oh, sorry sir. We don't serve liquor in our lodge," he said to my displeasure.

"Here goes my waking up in the morning as a new person," I thought to myself.

I finished my dinner as planned and was about to leave, when Mr Alex transpired and told me, "Sir, please ensure you sit out tonight for some time and watch. It is a beautiful experience, and I am sure you wouldn't have experienced anything like this in your life. Though it is full moon today, and that light is quite good, you carry a torch from us so that you can locate some animals during the night."

I nodded very interested, but in my mind, I knew I would hardly be able to keep myself awake after a while. After dinner, I began to walk back to my room, and it came to me then that my room was a long distance away from the reception area, and I was the only guest there. It didn't make me feel any easy, but I continued to walk in the dark, guessing my path.

Once I was in the room, I shrugged away the unease and went in to sleep. It was thoroughly uncomfortable that the weather was warm and there was no air conditioner or cooler in the room, which meant I had to make do with the ceiling fan. I had hardly put my head on the pillow when deep slumber overtook me.

I woke up with a start, and tried to calm myself down. I had hardly ever woken up with a start this way before, which made me wonder what the reason was. I honestly couldn't remember a nightmare. Though like most of us, I don't remember the complete thing I have dreamt, at least fragments would have come to me. But no, I surely hadn't woken up because of any nightmare.

"Strange," I told myself and put my head back on the pillow, and then I heard it. In the off-season, the dried leaves from the forest had become a layer of carpet, and in the quiet of the night, I heard the crunching of the leaves. I could hear it very clearly and hence understood that the movement was very near to my room. I had unconsciously stopped breathing, worried that the something outside the room would end up hearing it. I had to tell myself that it was not a big deal, and it was a forest area, and thus it was only natural that some or the other animal would be walking around. I told myself that if there was any such danger I perceived, it was a simple matter of giving a call to someone from the staff and they would attend to me without any delay. But then, the realisation crept over me slower than the noise I heard again of the dry leaves being walked on, that I didn't have a single individual's number from the lodge, except that of the fixed landline from the reception, and I remember the receptionist had closed down the desk immediately after dinner.

As I was busy trying to device an escape plan, within the periphery of my vision, I swear I saw something move near the window. There was nothing by the time I turned to look. Each of my hair strands was in attention position, as panic gripped me from within and from the outside.

I surely heard something move just outside in the veranda, and I could no longer breathe properly, and began to inhale and exhale from my mouth. I comprehended for the first time in my life what people meant when they said they could hear their own heart beat.

My mind was overactive and I was in a spree of scolding myself, "Forest! You wanted to come and spend time in a forest of all places. All alone that too! What were you thinking, you stupid fool!"

All hopes were lost when there was a faint sound at the door, as I cringed with fear.

"Sir," was what the creature spoke.

My logical mind hung on to it, and knew that this was a human form outside for sure. "Yes," I said faintly.

"You awake, sir? It is Mahesha."

I had half a mind to take the chair in the room and as I opened the door, hit it on Mahesha's head for making me panic this way. "What's with you, man? What were you trying to do?"

"Eh...nothing sir. I came and shouted your name for a couple of times, but there was no response. I thought for a moment, and came to the window to see if there are any lights on, but there weren't any. So before I go, I thought I will give you one final shout."

"But what's the issue? Why are you disturbing me in the middle of the night?"

"Huh...It is just ten in the night now."

"Oh! Is it? Hmm...okay. But still, what do you want?"

"Nothing sir. Alex sir had told me that you wanted to spend the night outside watching animals, and I should have given the torch. I forgot when you had come there. So I thought I will give it to you now."

"Come on man!" I exclaimed.

There was an odd screeching noise from the forest that again was very close from where we were standing, and I gripped the door for support. "What…what was that?" I asked drenched in fear.

"Hmm…it is deer, but they give out this sound only when they spot some other wild animal," he said in a casual note, as if he had high tea with wild animals every other day.

He beamed the torch light at the forest, and I must say it covered a good range. I could see up to a long distance, and we both spotted an assembly of deer, and all of them were looking in one direction, as one of them let out that same cry again.

Mahesha followed that gaze and only when the light reached almost the other corner, did we see something black.

"Shit! It's a panther, is it?" I asked ready to pull him in and close the door.

"No sir, it is just a bear. Why do you look so scared?" He asked. That brought in some respite to my scared self.

"It is nothing to be scared of. I am telling you that I have been working here for years now. It is a good experience. You must sit outside," he suggested.

"Bear, is it?" I said, breathing quite normally by then. My sleep had evaporated and I was contemplating to take the offer.

"If you want, I will sit with you for some time," he offered.

"Yes, that would be good." I got two chairs put out in the veranda.

On his suggestion, I had put off the light in the veranda, which he said was essential for ensuring we don't distract the animals. Mahesha kept scanning the area every few minutes with the powerful torch to see if there were any animals that we could spot, but visibly there were none.

There was a great improvement in my heart rate, which was going out of scale only minutes ago, and was now back to normal. I began to yawn again, and thought we should call it a day.

Once when Mahesha was focusing the light sideways, I asked him, "The forest continues on that side?"

"No sir. That is the common public road."

"You mean, someone can just come in if they get through the electric fence?" I asked.

"That's true sir, but no one comes here. You don't need to worry. It is quite deserted."

"Dude, shouldn't I be more worried that it is deserted? I mean, I am the only person in the lodge, that's situated far off from civilisation."

Mahesha didn't answer, but stopped the scanning torch once it reached thick growth of bamboos, and observed some movement and said, "Hey that's a Malabar squirrel." He pointed out happily, thrilled for having spotted at least something.

"What's a Malabar squirrel?" I asked disinterested.

"It is a big squirrel sir. It's been quite some time since I had seen one. Come sir, let's check out."

"What? Where?"

"It is a beautiful creature sir. Let's watch it up close."

"No! Wait, Mahesha!"

He was extremely enthusiastic and wouldn't listen.

"It is not dangerous, sir," he had reached the electric fence.

"Dude, there was a bear there just a while ago."

"Sir, since when did the bear start becoming dangerous?" he asked.

I was ashamed for I didn't know the answer. Sandhya, on the other hand, when we were seeing each other, had usually given me good counsel to watch National Geographic or at least The Animal Planet many times. But I had never gone beyond any of the music channels.

"Of course Mahesha, what do you think I am? I obviously am aware that bears are not dangerous. These are no polar bears that we need to be scared about," I put the point back to him.

"Then?" he questioned.

"The electric fence my friend, is quite dangerous!" I pointed out to him.

"Yes yes, sir. That I am aware of. I would not have taken you past the electric fence without switching the unit off," he said and went several steps further to open a switch board and turned off the unit.

"Now is it safe to enter?" I asked.

He didn't wait to answer me. Instead, he slid through the many wires that the fence was made of and asked me to follow him. I am sure you would appreciate that despite knowing that the main units are switched off, it is still not a very pleasant feeling to cross an electric fence.

"Come," he said and started to jog. I half ran and half jogged not to be left behind him. We were a good distance into the forest, as he tried to beam the torch light onto the thick set of bamboos. He could not track anything.

"You said you saw it!"

"Yes sir, I saw it with my own eyes," he exaggerated. He searched again for several minutes. I could only hear lot many types of beetles present in the forest, but there was no Malabar or Manappuram or Josallukas squirrel that we found.

"Let's leave this Malabar squirrel alone and go back."

"It was right here sir, I promise."

"No doubt about it Mahesha, but amidst these thick bushes, we might not be able to locate it. And think about it, we took time to reach here, right? It might have jumped off elsewhere," I said, and started to walk towards the fence.

I turned back to see Mahesha had switched off the torch.

"What's wrong with you, dude? Please switch on the torch."

"Ahem...sir the battery has died I think," he said in a low voice.

"Unbelievable man! Who asked you to keep wasting the charge on the useless squirrel? Now how do we get back?"

"The moonlight is quite bright sir. No worries. I will take you," he said.

"Meow."

We heard a cat.

"Wait, there's some kitty around. I will try to switch on my cell phone's torch."

"Eh...sir, let's leave."

"Why?"

"This is not a domestic cat."

"Meaning?"

"This is how a wild cat calls out," he said.

"What the f..! Is it carnivorous?"

"Yes!"

"God!" We ran towards the electric fence at a speed unknown to Raj-kind. Another 'meaaooww' came our way and it was quite near.

We scraped through the electric fence, and ran towards my room in the moonlight, having no time to switch on the torch in my phone.

"Idiot! What's wrong with you Mahesha? Shouldn't you know the ways of the jungle? You kept saying it is not dangerous," I said after I switched on the veranda lights and was sure that there was no cat, wild or otherwild.

He was puffing, "Sorry sir, it is not so dangerous. But you know it is carnivorous, and in case it has other cats with it..." he didn't have to complete it to make his point.

"Let's get into my room. You can sleep there tonight."

"No sir. I will go to the staff sleeping room."

"Don't be stupid, Mahesha."

"Not like that sir. I need to call my girlfriend before I sleep." He tried to blush even in such a situation.

"That reminds me, please share your phone number with me."

"Oh! You didn't have? Please take my number and call me if you need anything."

"Yes, I will. Now go quickly."

He jogged towards the staff quarters, and I couldn't see him after a distance. On reflex, I turned back to see if there was any animal, but thankfully there was nothing. "And then there were none," I said aloud inspired by Agatha Christie's book with the same title that I was planning to finish during these couple of days. I tried to calm down, and then the veranda light went off!

"Are you kidding me guys! Power cut, even here?" I rushed to my room immediately. I then observed that the lights in the room were working. I figured out that maybe there was some central line for all veranda lights, which this idiot Mahesha had switched off.

I went to the door, and remembered that I had not just bolted, but also locked the door. Exactly the point where I heard the rustling of the leaves. It had become windy, and if I could hear something like that, it was obvious that it came from a nearby place. I had no intention to wait for that thing to reach me, and quickly reached out to the key and tried opening the door, but it would just not open. I realised that maybe I was being very nervous and doing things in haste. I tried to compose myself and giving my mind a false sense of security that nothing could happen to me, the way I do in office when the numbers don't tally, I tried it again in an utmost delicate manner. It just would not open! I tried to focus the faint light from my cell phone on it, and saw that it was my bike's keys!

I heard the rustling again, and lost my cool. I tried Mahesha's phone number, "Where on earth is my room's key, Mahesha?"

"Sir, I don't know."

"Then please come running back. There is something nearby."

"Wait sir, did you leave the keys near the window where you had placed your chair?" he asked, and I put my hand near that window pane, and thank god he was right.

I got in and closed the door immediately, heaving a sigh of relief. "This much for a relaxing weekend," I said out loud. I thought that all was behind me now and I should just calm down and have a good night's sleep.

I could indeed still hear the crackling of the dry leaves, but my nerves had gotten used to it. I thought practically that there is no animal whatsoever that can open the door or break any windows to get in.

I made the bed again, and was about to switch off the lights, when a thought occurred to me. "Yes, it's true that no animal can break open the door or the windows, but what if there are some burglars?" My right brain, I tell you. It was over compensating to put all its creative imagination into play, as if it was a once-in-a-life-time opportunity for it to showcase its talent.

With what Mahesh had told me, there was one side of the lodge that faced the public road and anyone who could cross the electric fence, could easily come to his room.

"Thank god for electric fence..." Yes, you are right. I too realised it by the end of the sentence. "I don't think Mahesha turned the electric fence on again!"

"But relax Raj, all's well. Tell me how can a burglar just come in when the door is locked and the windows are also closed?" I asked myself, and moved the curtains once from the windows.

"What!" There were no iron rods protecting the window space! It was just a sheet of glass that stood between a probable intruder and me in the room. For all I knew, maybe I was being watched right now.

I switched off all the lights, so that no one could see me from outside, and observed that the sound of the leaves rustling had changed. I immediately called up Mahesha to shout out for help. But his number was busy, and guess what? He had not enabled the 'call waiting' option in his phone either, which meant he didn't even know I was trying to call him!

I scanned through the room for any probable weapons that I might need to have with me in case there was an intruder. In a matter of minutes I had figured out that there was nothing in the room worth using as a weapon of destruction. I tried to search my luggage and the only thing that could be classified anywhere close to a 'weapon' was the nail clipper that I had, with a soda bottle opener. I was sure the burglar would not come for any manicure or to have wine with me, for this lodge didn't have any liquor whatsoever. I found a miniature pair of scissors in the end. I didn't know if it could be of any great use, but thanked Leonardo Da Vinci nevertheless for this brilliant invention, for it gave me a little confidence to walk around the room at least.

Every minute passed like an hour. I sat on the bed looking at the two possible entry points through the window and almost waited thinking someone would break the glass and would just enter. I cleared my throat thinking if that happened, I could shout so loudly that the people sleeping in the staff room far away should be able to hear me and come to my rescue. But the chances were bleak. Only the Malabar squirrel or that wild cat nearby would hear me, and I don't think those were contemplating on coming to my rescue anyway.

I was sleepy now, but was too scared to even lie down. In an attempt to be safer, I placed some delicate glass and then some metal objects at the window sill thinking that in case someone managed to open the windows, these objects could at least create enough noise for me to prepare for the fight with that someone with my miniature scissors. I tried calling Mahesha again, but his cell was switched off. I had a very light sleep for a few hours the whole night, where I kept waking up in between, hearing strange noises. I was relieved to hear a cock crowing after several uneasy hours, and only then did I sleep for some time. I woke up when there was daylight, and packed up with no intention of staying there another night.

At breakfast, Mr Alex came down, "Good morning Mr Raj. I heard you have decided to leave a day earlier. Please stay one more day as per schedule."

"No thanks, Mr Alex. I need to leave for Bangalore now. I've got some work to do."

"Hmm...that's sad. And, tell me how was the night?" he asked.

I tried to smile and said, "Exactly how you said Mr Alex. It was nothing like I'd experienced in my life ever before." And he went back looking content.

I left that place to ride back very slowly to Bangalore. I was fatigued and woke up with a temperature the next day and this lasted for a few days and I couldn't go to office.

Now that I have told you the real reason for me falling sick, you understand why I am taken aback by Pramod's and perhaps his girlfriend's take on idolising me.

As he'd promised, Pramod emailed me the contact details and in fact a scanned copy of a certain leaflet having details pertaining to this particular project.

The initial reaction was that it was too good a deal. With earlier experiences, I would not think of any such good thing till I verified each aspect of the deal. Then I saw that the location mentioned was near Electronic City, and hence not too far away from my office. The excitement then got to me. Pramod also had mentioned in the mail that the last twelve plots were remaining out of the one hundred and seventy-five that were formed and released for booking two months ago. That was some great speed of conversion, and while I have learnt not to blindly trust people, Pramod had given me reasons to believe that come what may, he would not bluff me on such issues. So I decided to take it at face value. Which also meant that I needed to act quickly and maybe visit this place soon. Waiting for my father over the weekend would mean delay and loss of precious time. So I immediately took permission to leave early, after having to convince my supervisor that I was not going to attend any interviews with competitors.

You wouldn't believe that the address was quite easy to locate, and once I looked through the property thoroughly, I almost had the pinewood kind of excitement trying to grow in me. But as you all are aware, once bitten twice shy, I had made up my mind to see what loopholes there were. I could find none. It was time to inform my father now to do his round. Though I was really tempted to call off sick the next day and come to the location with my father, I didn't want to cause unnecessary suspicion at work. So I updated my father about it, and we agreed to visit that place over the upcoming weekend.

My dad walked from one corner of the project to the other, and seemed to be in a state of disbelief. "Something is not adding up, Raj," he said, seemingly having reached a stalemate in his mind.

"I understand what you are saying, Dad. But even I could not put my finger to it."

"You know, if you look at all the advertisements in the papers for this area, the prices are much higher. In fact, this is quite close to Electronic City, and hence the prevailing market value should be at least forty percent higher in my view."

"Okay Dad, let's try to check the list of all the issues we have had."

"Bhairaveshwara and Basaveshwara confusion?"

"Nope, this is the exact location. I risked calling Pramod and he's verified it. He's sent me a picture of the plot he has already registered. It is right here, two rows to the left."

"East-west confusion is not an issue. Also this cost is something you will be able to afford without even going to a bank for the loan, of course assuming that Mr Nair will return your money. Remind me we need to follow up with Mrs Anu next week. So even cost is not a show-stopper then." He was still wondering.

"Did you see the branded apartments visible from the main gates of this property Dad?"

"Exactly."

"So what do you say Dad? Do we proceed?"

"No, not yet Raj. When something looks too good to be true, it is usually just that – too good to be true. Let me rake my brains a little once I go home. Don't commit to anything till we are completely convinced."

"But Dad, there are only twelve plots remaining. At least that was the news a few days ago. I am not sure if these will remain untaken for long."

"I understand Raj. I am not saying we will sit idle and waste our time. I just want to be sure of what we are doing. Let's take a walk outside the gates."

"What? Why?"

"Come."

We walked and walked, until he was puffing, getting out of breath. He had put on his hat to cover himself from the warm afternoon. He seemed to have made a few quick decisions, and asked me to go get the bike to where he stood, while he would speak to a few people around.

It was half a kilometre's walk back for me, and I returned with my bike in some time. By then my Dad was seemingly tired and was perspiring slightly.

As soon as I approached, he said, "No Raj, something is surely amiss. You see that we have come further from the main connectivity roads. That simply means the value of the properties here should either reduce or at the least remain the same. However, as I'd guessed, there is an increase in the prices of the property by at least twenty percent."

"Oh, is it?" I was surprised.

"We saw at least three branded apartments in this half a kilometre, and each one is priced exorbitantly. Then again, I found out that there are two more developers who have launched projects on plots. And they are costlier."

"But couldn't it be the same issue we saw with Pinewoods and Enclave? There was a big difference between each one's value propositions."

"No Raj, it is not a like to like comparison. Understand that those were plain lands somewhere in the outskirts. But here you have apartments that have already come up and also the connectivity is excellent. You cannot have too wide a difference. Let's get back on this. Let me think. Give me the developer's contact details."

"Sure Dad, here."

I gave him all the details that I had received from Pramod, as I had carried additional printed copies with me. I also added, "If what I hear from Pramod is right, at least four people, from his circle have blocked plots here. I can get their details if needed. So many people won't make the same mistake, right Dad?"

"I will talk to you in a day or two, Raj." My Dad was not in a mind-set to be convinced at all. I thought that my Dad was over-reacting.

▲

Pramod came to me directly the next day, "Raj, I hope you will close out your decision soon man. I am not trying to worry you, but I get that there were some of my friends' friends who visited the property yesterday. They were looking at investing in this area, and if I know them well; if one of them decides to invest, the others will follow suit. Just thought I should give you this heads up."

It was actually nice of him to convey these details to me. It only made my situation worse though. I was having difficulty in closing just a few items on which I sat the whole day. I got a call from my father, which was a bit of silver lining to me, and he said he wanted to meet me.

"But Dad, you know it is difficult for me to travel during weekdays."

"Yes, so I am already on the way. I will reach your room in an hour or so. Will you be able to reach by then?"

"Oh Dad, who asked you to travel all by yourself?"

"Okay Raj, I cannot hear what you are talking properly. See you in an hour."

He is quite clever in invoking the BSNL signal issue as and when he does not want to hear something. I left to reach home.

"Here, listen..." Dad said after he reached and as soon as we settled down. "Here's the story. So I went to the sub-registrar's office to understand the history of the land under consideration. Everything seemed to be fine, and all legality considered. The hand-over from one party to the other, spanning up to few decades were all captured accurately and there is nothing to be suspicious about, except one thing," he paused.

"Yes Dad, shoot."

"So you gave me this number stating this belongs to the developer, right? I gather that he is a reseller and not the developer"

"Hmm...didn't understand. How does it matter?"

"Ideally it may not. But I kind of found it fishy. On asking around, I understand that this land was supposed to be a project for people from backward communities and minorities. That was when the original developer would have done mass registrations, etc. However, it looks like many wanted to resell their land. The representative is the one whose number Pramod has shared."

"You mean, out of all the plots, only some of them wanted to resell it for their individual profit. Thus, it is possible that they got the land at a much cheaper rate and now want to sell it at a higher price and use the money for something else."

"That's correct."

"Cool then, but where's the issue Dad? I mean isn't this a win-win situation?"

"See Raj, this is a business transaction, and yes you are right in saying that legally all seems fine. But you need to weigh in all the pros and cons before making the decision."

"But I don't see any cons."

"Well, if in case any of the people who have now agreed to resell it, tomorrow want to create an issue and want to claim their rightful land back, then you will be in trouble."

"What does that mean Dad? We would have already got their consent and necessary signatures in the right places, no?"

"See Raj, technically you are right. However, there's always subjectivity involved in court decisions. Let's assume for a moment that someone has threatened these land-owners from backward communities and has made them agree to resell it to people like us. If tomorrow the same suppressed individual wakes up to is right, the court will uphold the decision in his or her favour. Are you getting what I am saying?"

"Hmmm... Yes Dad. This is very tricky."

"True. Hence, if you want to take a risk and buy this property, think very carefully about it. In no situation do I want to see you running around for court cases, and worse, losing all your investments if you lose your case."

"So hypothetically, if someone wants to create an issue even if none was threatened, then considering the overall sensitivity, the court may still go against us and thus uphold the right of an underprivileged individual?"

"Precisely worded!"

"I just..." I was frustrated to find any words to describe my feelings. "Is this how difficult it is to get a piece of land, Dad?"

"I understand what you are going through, Raj. Keep faith. There are several more options to look at."

"Umm...I don't know. I think we can now move on to the paper cut-outs"

"No, before that, let me tell you that I got an invitation for a wedding in Nelamangala town."

"What?"

"We will go to that wedding this weekend is what I wanted to tell you."

"But Dad, we were just talking about land, and without warning you are jumping to a wedding topic."

"No, hear me out. It is a family friend who had come home to invite us for the wedding. And I happen to know from him that Nelamangala is quite a happening place now in terms of acquiring land."

"Why would you talk to some random person about our interest in acquiring a plot of land Dad?"

"I didn't go chasing him to tell me about any land availability, sonny boy. He just happened to complain how difficult it was getting with many reaching out to him for details pertaining to land value in his place. He is a known name in his district, considering he is the chairman of certain community groups. Hence, because of his strong network, many come to him to take advice either to sell or buy property it seems."

"Hmm...sounds reasonable. So did he say something that helps us?"

"I took from him a couple of promoters' numbers. I will contact them during the week."

"Okay." I yawned, tired and leaned on the easy chair that belonged to our previous generation, deep in thought if Nelamangala was the place where I will land up buying a piece of land.

"But why Nelamangala of all places?" I asked Byrappa, the family friend who had visited my father to invite us for his daughter's wedding. I usually don't talk to family friends, especially elders, in this tone, but something had got into me.

"Why Yelahanka?" he asked in return.

"Meaning?"

"Why Jalahalli? Why HSR layout?" he continued.

"What are you saying, Uncle?"

"These are the kind of questions people were asking a decade or fifteen years ago son. Now you know that you cannot even afford any plot in these very places. I myself had a plot of land in Bommanahalli, near HSR layout. I invested money to construct a duplex as well back in the early nineties. My house was the first one to be constructed in the whole of neighbourhood. Do you not remember being there for the house warming ceremony when you were in lower primary?"

As a matter of fact, I did remember. It was literally the only house in the neighbourhood at least a kilometre away from the main road. I remember vaguely that there was a small lake nearby. "Yes, I remember now, Uncle. It was the one near the lake where me and my cousins went to catch small fish in metal containers, right?"

"Tadpoles!"

"Excuse me?"

"You had got tadpoles in those containers thinking they were fish."

"Eww...Really? Anyway, so I do remember the house."

"Neither my wife nor my kids wanted to move to that house considering it was very far off from the city. You know that my wife was a government servant back then and had to travel from the city bus stand till this house and it was not considered safe. I had to sell the house off in a year and used that money to buy another house in Nelamangala, which is where my wife's office was. Today, do you know the rates in Bommanahalli?"

"I assume it is costly."

"I sold the house for hardly anything, and today even if I want to buy back my own house, and willing to pay more than ten times the value I sold it at, I am not able to. Do you understand?"

"Okay what is the rate in Nelamangala, Uncle? I will take a decision accordingly."

"See Raj, you are like my son. I have taken a few plots in Nelamangala myself for investment purpose. I am also the chairman of a few groups, and getting a piece of land for me is not a big deal. I will show you all my plots, and you choose from them. You come this weekend to the town."

"But Uncle, isn't it your daughter's marriage in a week's time."

"Come on son. Marriages can wait, the plot of land cannot. Hurry up."

"That's so nice of you, Uncle. What would be the cost of the property? I need to know in case I need to raise loan amount."

"You are not listening Raj. I told you that you are like my son," and he smiled.

"That's fine, Uncle, but how much do I need to pay?"

He just smiled.

"You mean Uncle…"

"For you, I will give it for free. What will I do with four plots at my age?"

"Wow Uncle! Thank you so much. When I construct a house there, I will name it 'Byrappa enclave' Uncle. Thank you so much."

"Come on son. Can I not do even so much for you? Just ensure you come to my daughter's wedding without fail and give her your blessings."

"Absolutely Uncle, it goes without saying." My father was pulling at my shoulder, which was disturbing my conversation with Byrappa Uncle.

"Dad wait, I am talking..." but my father nudged my shoulder forcefully, and I woke up on the easy chair that once belonged to my grandfather. "Where is Byrappa Uncle? Wait, was it just a dream?"

"You were snoring so badly Raj. Byrappa Uncle? He is in Nelamangala, busy with his daughter Mangala's marriage. Was he in your dreams?"

"Oh crap Dad!"

"What happened? Was it a nightmare? Byrappa can look scary in reality, so I won't be surprised if his appearance scared you in your dreams."

"No Dad, he was giving me a free plot of land."

"Ha! Byrappa and a free plot of land! You call me stingy. Byrappa's stinginess is several times greater than mine." He smiled.

"Is it?" I asked, still adjusting my eyes to the illumination in the room.

"Even if you had married his daughter, he would not have given you any free piece of land. It is our luck that he doesn't charge us for his advice."

"Why will I marry his daughter? I will only marry Sa..." I stopped, coming to my senses quickly said, "I will only marry someone from this city."

I hoped that my father hadn't got a hint.

"Good, at least you are talking about your marriage yourself. Do I need to start searching for a girl or you will do it yourself?"

"Dad!"

"What?"

"Let's first get our hands around a plot. I will let you know about my marriage later. I will let you search for someone."

"That is sad to know."

"Eh...what?"

"I thought you will have at least zeroed in on someone."

"No Dad, I would not relieve you from your duties that way. I will leave the complete responsibility of searching for a girl on you. But that is the next project. For now, let's focus on project 'plot of land'."

"Fair, I agree. Let me then shortlist some properties so that we can visit them while we're in Nelamangala."

"Tell me one thing, Dad."

"Hmm..."

"There was this house that Byrappa Uncle owned in Bommanahalli right, and then he sold it."

My Dad stopped on his tracks. "Not bad at all. You remember it? You were very young then. Yes, he sold it long back to buy a house in Nelamangala."

"I think it is a sign, Dad."

"What?"

"I am confident of finding something good in Nelamangala."

"A good plot you mean?"

"Wottaplot!"

"Eh...Okay, you mean 'what a plot?'"

"No Dad, it is 'wottaplot!'. As soon as you look at the property, you must say 'wottaplot!' with excitement."

"Something like that Pinewoods we saw when we had begun our search?"

"Hmm...not exactly. Close, but not exactly."

"Let's see son. We will hope for the best."

I spent some time trying to recollect the fragments of my dream. Today, there was no way a middle class man could buy any property in main Bangalore. So if we at least invest in the outskirts, tomorrow the value and as well as the amenities would surely be much better. I have myself passed through Bommanahalli sometimes, and could relate to the vast development it has seen in these years. What Byrappa Uncle said in my dream was right.

For some reason I felt very vibrant and positive when we had to go to Nelamangala. It was the land calling me. We planned to go early in the morning, to see if we could finish looking at the properties before the wedding that was scheduled after noon.

Nagesh, an agent who worked with a couple of promoters and nominated by Byrappa Uncle to help us out, was right on time at the said spot to accompany us. I went to him and shook his hand and nodded, "Nagesh". I kept shaking his hand and nodding for several seconds, which I realised was making him uncomfortable. So I released my vicious grip. He had come in his VTS 50, the moped that was launched, if I'm not mistaken, in early 1980s.

Nagesh was one of the puniest chaps in Nelamangala town. But when he sat on the moped, it seemed to fit him just right. As if it was made for him, or wait, considering the vintage model of the moped, maybe he was born for that.

He started the moped and we followed him on my bike. It was the slowest riding I had ever done in my life. I could not even move to second gear as we followed him. I did however, appreciate his confidence in riding at that speed in the middle of the road. None of the other commuters dared to challenge him by honking. They all subtly overtook him without wanting to disturb him, though they'd honked crazily at me just before.

He seemed to know half the town, and more than half the town seemed to know him, for there were few waves and several salutes thrown at him from others around. It was clear that we were in esteemed company. One of the locals shouted out offering Nagesh, "Sir, come have tea with us", to which Nagesh gently waved saying he will join some other day. I was extremely tempted to say that we might as well ask that individual to serve tea, as I was sure that with the speed that we were traveling, tea could have been prepared, served, had, and then I could have returned to find Nagesh with his VTS 50 right after fifty metres from where I'd left him.

The amount of residual smoke his moped was releasing was surely colouring my face grey, through the helmet I wore. In fact, I had all the time in the world to observe that the colour and the texture of the smoke. This was indeed VTS 50's shades of grey! Something that was done in the 1980s in India, whereas the world got to know about the other fifty shades only decades later.

Once I got bored of identifying the different shades of the smoke, I looked on either sides of the road while riding (Statutory warning: Do not perform this stunt of looking around while riding your bike, as it was done here under strict supervision of my father, and non-standard riding conditions at a speed of eight kmph with other vehicles giving way for Nagesh's moped unconditionally) to find that the day begins a bit late in the town. People were relatively chilled out in life and went about their chores without any hurry. In fact, even the sun chose to wake up a bit later in this town (Of course, it's exaggerated folks. It just fits in well here), as the glares from the big one wasn't sharp as yet. Nature, I saw, is best appreciated when you are out of Bangalore, in a small town, looking around while riding at a speed of eight kmph.

A helmet, as a strict rule, was a no-no here. In fact, only after riding for a good fifteen minutes, by which I mean, after covering half a kilometre, is when I saw that none of the folks on bikes wore helmets. No wonder people didn't miss giving me a stare. Initially, when some college girls smiled at me as I passed by, I mistook it to be admiration, and only now it hit me that they were perhaps laughing at me for wearing a helmet.

People like Nagesh are stout sponsors of making Nelamangala a helmet free zone, for even he didn't wear one, and seeing that he was a household name in half of Nelamangala, his fans would again follow him by riding free-headed. It surely needs to be observed that if people ride at the speed that Nagesh was riding, then I will personally join the rally to make this town a helmet free zone, for there was no question of accidents happening.

In my reverie, I had made the mistake of not observing that the moped had further reduced speed. Only when my Dad hit my shoulder asking me to look in the front did I see that Nagesh's moped had almost come to a stop. I had to hit the brakes to ensure I didn't run into him.

I was of the opinion that he would be stopping the moped near some property, but this was a busy street, where even at the relatively early hour by the town standards, I could see people moving about. I could not fathom the reason for him coming to an abrupt halt. It was also a narrow street and not easy to park the bike.

As I waited for him to at least turn around and tell us the reason, a man from the nearby hotel came out in a hurry greeting Nagesh in an exaggerated manner. After they exchanged details of how each family member was in terms of health and fitness, Nagesh turned around and said, "This is Maani. He is the owner of this Udupi hotel."

Both my father and I greeted him.

"His hotel prepares the best idli and sambar in the whole of South Nelamangala. Every child in this locality knows who is Udupi Hotel Maani," Nagesh patted Mr Maani's back, as we said something supposedly pleasant.

I added saying, "The way the same kids would know who Nagesh is I presume," which I don't think they heard amidst their chit-chat.

Nagesh turnaround and asked, “Huh?”

Thinking that it may not have been the best of observations to let him know, I just shook my head smilingly.

Nagesh immediately got off the moped, with the keys still in it, and started to walk with Mr Maani. I was a bit zapped and didn’t know what to do. Was I supposed to just wait for them to finish catching up with the local gossip and return? Was I needed to take care of his moped from being stolen, for the keys were still in it?

Thankfully, I didn’t have to make any decision, as Nagesh finally decided to turn around before entering the hotel and announced, “What are you doing there Raj and Setty sir? Please join in,” and went in.

I was looking around to know how or where to park my bike and guess was taking a lot of time. Nagesh returned to check.

“What happened, Raj?”

“Eh...There is no place to park around. Let me go further down the lane and return after parking,” I got up, asking my Dad to join the others.

“There is so much place to park here. Haven’t I parked already?”

“You mean...I just leave the vehicle here? It might disturb the other commuters.”

Even Mr Maani had joined in by now, and they started laughing at me, the way elders laugh at kids at their folly.

I didn’t say much, and understood that I was just supposed to leave the bike there, and join the rest. Mr Maani excitedly slapped my arm, for the obvious entertainment I had provided, which physically hurt a lot. But I was cognizant of the fact that I just had to as much as reach my arm to rub it, and there will be another fit of laughter from the other end. Quick learner, we call it in our BPO, where folks just pick stuff up looking at just one protocol and run with the rest in a smooth manner.

Anyway, before entering the hotel, I tapped on Nagesh's shoulder. Half the folks sitting in the hotel turned to look at me, perhaps waiting for just a word from Nagesh to bring out all the metallic weapons that they'd hid under their respectable attire. But the stars were on my side this morning, including the sun that was shining bright right into my eyes. Nagesh smiled, and the paused hustle bustle regained momentum, as they now knew that I was a mere tapper of the shoulder and I meant no harm to their mass leader.

"Yes Raj?" he asked gently.

Being a kind soul that I am (I say this to myself for no one else seems to realise it. They just don't look deep enough obviously), I offered my help to Nagesh, "I will lock your moped and return in a jiffy."

There was a bigger roar of laughter in the hotel, including those with the hidden metal weaponry. Mr Maani held on to his pot belly as he laughed, and also took support from the nearby table to avoid falling on the floor. Nagesh looked hither thither laughing, basking in the attention he got from the crowd, as he shook his head funnily.

"Raj Raj Raj," said he. This was a worrisome way of addressing someone. Firstly, I was quite confident that I was the only Raj around in this hotel. Yes, I know I had said that mine is the most common name ever in history, but my author has informed me that he has placed no other guy in this hotel with the same name to avoid confusion. If there was any other Raj in the hotel, it would have been quite possible that with my average looks, the other Raj then might end up being considered as the protagonist of this story. So hence, the theory that I was the only Raj present in the hotel was right. Thus it was a surprise why Nagesh would call out the name three times.

Secondly, I asked myself, "See Raj, I have a general knowledge question for you. Tell me the name of the place where someone's name is repeated for three times?" Unfortunately, I knew that the answer was the court of law. I only hoped that there was no parallel law and order that ran in this town, where I would be made to stand in the victim box and sentences will be called out for some wrong that I had done without meaning. Was I not supposed to offer locking Nagesh's moped? Or is it that in this part of the world, you are given sentences after having laughed at for such minor lapse in manners?

"What Raj..." said Mr Maani, and continued, "Locking Nagesh's moped you say? Do you think anyone would start the moped?"

Ah! Now I understood. It was obvious to me now that I had received a faint hint, thanks to Udupi Hotel Maani. This was an age old model of a moped, guys! Even if someone wanted to start and scoot away, the technique of starting such an old model was not a joke. It required vintage criminals to do it. And we all know that even if someone managed to start the vehicle to steal it, people could just jog behind and catch the criminal. I now joined in with them and started to laugh as well.

"Who dares to touch Nagesh's moped? They all know the consequences," said Mr Maani, as I gulped heavily. So much for being a quick learner.

I went to Nagesh, and tried to word my sentence such that he did not take offence, "So Nagesh, eh...In case we get late, will we be able to cover all the properties? I mean, can we come back to Mr Maani's hotel once we are done with seeing all the properties?"

"There is a rule in this area Raj, that we are not supposed to pass Udupi Hotel without having the idlies dipped in hot sambar. I am telling you Raj, you would not have tasted such idlies ever in your life."

I did want to ask him if there was any exception approval that could be exercised for such a rule, for we had come here to see some property, but with the swiftness he showed in disappearing into the hotel's sitting area, which was dead opposite to the swiftness at which his vehicle travelled, I decided to join in.

It was a sort of blessing in disguise, as we had hardly had a few slices of bread before leaving home in the morning. Nagesh, I must say, had an excellent set of taste buds. My father and I were indulging in idlies, dipped in piping hot sambar, as if we had starved for days together.

After we were done destroying the idlies, I felt it was the right thing for us to do to order for hot cups of coffee. A south Indian tiffin cannot be considered complete without a hot cup of filter coffee. I waved at Mr Maani, who was busy behind the cashbox, and said, "Sir, three cups of hot coffee," and smiled.

I looked at Nagesh, to give him a knowing nod as to how I had read his mind, but he surprised me. "No Maani, we are very late. Cancel the coffee order," to which Mr Maani just nodded and got on with his work.

I didn't understand the reason Nagesh had done this. But it was true that we had spent a lot of time already in the hotel, so I didn't bother. My father and Nagesh were ahead of me. I stopped at the cash counter and reached out for my wallet, "How much was that, Mr Maani?" Again, roaring laughter from all nooks and corners for the hotel. I wouldn't be surprised, if this author had placed extras in the hotel just to make fun of me by laughing unnecessarily. Before anyone spoke to me, I understood that you don't get to pay anyone in Nelamangala when you have Nagesh by your side. My quick learner concept was taking quite a beating. I quickly placed the wallet in my pocket and ran to start my bike.

Nagesh clearly showed the need for urgency now, as he had upped the speed of his moped from eight kmph to twelve kmph, and thankfully I was getting to exercise my bike's second gear, which had caught some rust because of non-usage in the past hour or so.

There was a moment of glory when Nagesh's moped, because of the downhill side, touched the speed of twenty kmph, a record of sorts that he shall be proud of. But then he immediately turned to his left without any indication or anything, which baffled me. Maybe he didn't like it one bit that his bike had caught up so much speed and hence took a turn to get the normal twelve kmph speed back.

This road seemed to have a lot of open areas and I did see some advertising boards highlighting that there were plots for sale, which made my mood upbeat. Finally I will get to see some plots of my desire, I felt. Nagesh again just stopped the vehicle in the middle of the road. I had learned from the last two instances, and was now maintaining a good distance from his moped, so there was no possibility of me running into him. Also by now, I knew that people in Nelamangala, and especially Nagesh, do not use indicators to take a turn or stop the vehicle. He was like Rajinikanth of the area.

There was a not-so-great looking property in front of which Nagesh had stopped. I was a bit concerned, but then he looked to cross the road, and on following his gaze, I saw he seemed to be headed to another hotel. He saw the confusion on my face and smiled. I took it as a given that we were supposed to cross the road along with him.

On reaching the hotel, a man, again present at the cash counter, came running to Nagesh. "Oh ho! It's been very long since you visited my hotel, Nagesh. You seem to have got some guests with you. Please come, please come."

Once we were seated, Nagesh introduced us to the man, "Setty sir and Raj, this is Mahesh Maiya. He owns this hotel. Here is where we get the best *uddina vade* and coffee in the whole of South Nelamangala," and now things added up in my mind. I too wanted to play this game.

"Oh! Folks in my office have spoken about this hotel so much. It seems there's a rule in Nelamangala that we are not supposed to pass this road without having uddina vade and coffee of this hotel," I said excitedly, taking turns to look at Nagesh and Mr Maiya. Nagesh seemed to be at a loss of words, while the latter beamed with pride.

My dad, getting into the groove now said, "Even I have heard that we would not have had such uddina vade or coffee ever in our lives before," and winked at me.

Nagesh was extremely pissed that we were using all the lines that the author had kept aside for him. He obviously had no other lines, and hence he only nodded along, just smiling.

Again, we had to give it to Nagesh for having found good places for food in the nooks and corners of his town. I was hoping that he had put even half of such an effort in shortlisting the properties. We chatted with Mr Maiya for a bit while eating, as he briefed us about his family, and said that his son's name is Vedanth.

"That's a very nice name," I said, really meaning it.

"I thought that when we had named him that, Mr Raj. But it is not so."

"Why do you say that, sir? It is such a nice and rare name."

"Rare? Are you joking? So many boys of his age are named Vedanth," he cribbed.

"You mean to say Vedanth is the new Raj?" I was happy that there was some name that had now risen up to the occasion and was waiting to replace the name Raj from the number one spot.

"Eh...what?" Of course he didn't understand what I said and I didn't spend any more words on that topic, as we prepared to leave.

I didn't repeat any of my mistakes I did at Mr Maani's and let Nagesh pay Mr Maiya as we exited the hotel.

"So this is the stretch where we have a couple of properties that I will show, and there will be another route where we will find one more, which is actually on the way to the marriage hall. There are more than ten properties that I am aware of, but the remainder ones are not worth it in my view."

I was quite happy with the way he told us the parameters he'd used to shortlist these in terms of connectivity to Bangalore and to the centre of the town, the nearness of the plots to the main roads, the quality of developers he'd known on the basis of past experience and the future prospects each of these properties held. He then added, "I have intentionally not filtered any of the options on the basis of the price of the property. While it was also because I didn't know your budget, it was actually because there will be a lot of banks willing to give loans, and hence if you like a property, you can avail loans as well."

"That is a very good method Nagesh," my father stole my words, and I agreed with him enthusiastically.

We went down the same lane and stopped near one of the properties. "This is not a new property. All the plots from the initial stage are sold. However, one of the customers is in dire need for money because of personal reasons. Hence, he'd put a word to Byrappa sir, and he's given me the responsibility to find a buyer for this property."

I walked around in the area. Most of the amenities were all in place, and it was not very far from the main road either. I studied my own behaviour, and realised that I was searching for reasons to not buy the plot. I don't know if it was the point of resale that pricked me or what exactly, but I was not very convinced.

Nagesh was the blue-eyed boy of the town for a reason. While I thought that he would ask me for my opinion, he came to me and said, "Don't make any decision right away Raj. See all the plots and then think over it."

He then took us to another nearby property which had a pleasant feel about it. However, it was located some half a kilometre from the main road. Nagesh specifically quoted that it was the only drawback of the site. He mentioned that this distance from the main road is more than compromised with the rates that the promoter was quoting. Also he mentioned that unlike the one we saw before this, this was a direct launch from the promoters and was not a resale, which seemed to me to be a positive point.

"See Raj, if your intention is solely to invest money into a plot, and see it grow over the years, this is surely an option worth considering. However, if your intention is to get a plot where you want to settle down and construct a house, this might not be the best option."

"That's a good point, Nagesh."

"Also, I know the promoter well. Considering the plots are not selling like hot cakes because of the distance from the main road, he is willing to negotiate on the price. I can guarantee that if you have to get down to comparing this site with any other in this part of the town, this is surely the least costly one. As I said, there are loans available as well. In my experience, loans are much faster to get processed when it is a new property as against a resale one."

"Yes, Nagesh. This is quite alright," said my father. "Except for the distance from the main road, which is kind of already compensated for in the value quoted, rest of the points seem fine."

"The next one, and the last one I plan to show you today is a bit further from here, almost en-route Bangalore," he said, which caught our attention.

"Oh, so it also might be priced very differently?" my father checked.

"Agreed sir, but once let's take a look at it. In fact, it is difficult for me to get my moped till there. So I request you both to come with me to my house, and I will get my bike. It will be easier for me to travel long distance that way," he said, to which we both agreed readily.

On reaching his house, my father went in to freshen up a bit as well, so we had a brief pit-stop, where we were introduced to his family, including his two little twin daughters, who were very adorable.

I am no good with kids, and I think I also send out that simple vibe which ensures even kids don't come to me. But these twins were all over me, making me wonder what was happening. One of them wanted to take a selfie with me, and before I could get that done, the other wanted me to have a glass of water that she'd got for me from the earthen pot. My recently cut short hair was a matter of amusement to them, as one of them was trying to comb it for me. I had never in my life got so much attention from kids.

I was kicking myself for not having at least a couple of chocolates that I could give them. It was time for us to leave, and my father was hurrying me to join him, while I had a bit of difficulty parting from the two little gems. They were seemingly unhappy that I had to leave, but they behaved so well by just waving at me standing at a distance. I made a mental note to make some time and return to them someday soon.

Once we got to our bikes, I think I saw a different Nagesh. The speed at which he rode his bike was making it difficult to keep track of him. He was a changed man, with a helmet in place, and a jacket that was way cooler than mine, making me feel slightly jealous. Even his bike was of a better make, which I kept giving my dad as the reason for not being able to catch up with him on the road. He now used the indicator for every other turn he made. I mean he was using his indicator even to change lanes, which I never do. Like his kids, maybe even he had a twin which he had hidden from the world at large.

It was indeed a place slightly far from where we had already visited, and as he had said was nearer to both the wedding hall that we had to visit, as well as to Bangalore. He parked his bike very neatly, unlike his evil twin, and we went ahead to see the last of the plots.

It was on the main road and very easy to locate. All the items in the checklist for a good plot, this plot had. "It is as good as Pinewoods, right Dad?" I asked him, to which he nodded enthusiastically.

However, when my Dad heard the price, he seemed to reconsider his opinion. "That's very costly, Raj."

"But Dad, it is a good plot."

"Yes, but we need to consider all angles. I understand the point that the developer has amenities planned like we have in all the apartments in Bangalore. But this is very costly I feel."

"Dad, think about it long term. This is right across the main road. The connectivity is excellent. In a matter of months, the property value will increase and make up for the high price."

"Ok listen. If you like it so much, we surely will consider it. But don't make an immediate decision."

"We have come all the way from Bangalore to see this. I think we should finalise it soon."

"Hold on Raj, you are getting carried away. Nothing will happen if we don't close the decision immediately."

"Dad, please trust me. I have this sixth sense telling me that this is a brilliant proposition."

"Who is asking you to not consider it Raj? We will talk to Nagesh as well."

I don't think my Dad was getting my point. He was stuck with his old school of thought. "Dad, think about it. You used your method of judgement and got stuck with a bad plot, right? Let me make this decision please." I knew I should have been more sensitive about it, but I was very excited.

My Dad didn't show any signs of feeling bad, but then he didn't comment much after this.

"I think I like it a lot, Nagesh," I told him.

"What is your opinion about the other two?"

"I think all three are good, but this to me is by far the best."

"Good to know that. What about Mr Setty? What is his suggestion?"

My father didn't say much, "It is his decision, Nagesh."

"So what are the next steps, Nagesh?"

"I will talk to the developer and let you know Raj. But my friendly advice is that always sleep over it. You can make the decision tomorrow. There are lots of available plots in this project, and there's no hurry."

What's wrong with everyone? Why do they not understand that I am already done with my decision?

I was trying to form sentences in my mind to say to Nagesh to ensure I give the message without it coming out rudely the way I messed up while talking to my father a minute ago. But before I could say anything, my father asked Nagesh, "What is that work happening across on the other side of the road, Nagesh?"

"Sir, that is a big project that another developer is working on. It is still in the initial stages and they have not quoted any price. But when it comes up, it will have a lot of demand for sure."

"When is it due to come up?" asked my father.

"As it is a much bigger venture, there is still a lot of paperwork pending, sir. While the developers are telling everyone that it will be out in the next six months, I am confident that they will at least take a year."

I interrupted, "But why do you say it will have a lot of demand? Will it be better than this plot I have finalised?"

"So, from a development standpoint, I don't foresee that will be any better than this. But that project has been approved by the BMRDA, so it will surely sell out very soon."

"What? You mean this plot we are keen on isn't approved by the BMRDA?"

"No sir, this is a DC conversion site." These technical language was going over my head.

"Wait people, please. I am no expert like you both, but please help me with basic questions. So Nagesh, while this plot is not BMRDA approved, will there be any big difference in the market value because of that? Either now or in the future?"

"In the past, BDA or BMRDA approved sites used to surely command a premium over the others. However, being involved in this field now for some years, I am seeing it becoming an equal playing field. But the point that cannot be ignored is that people still have this inclination to go for BMRDA sites versus DC converted, though it will be a very small difference."

"That's okay with me," I said bluntly and shrugged, but my Dad wasn't done.

"But then Nagesh, there is no issue as such for loan availability between the two, right?"

"No issues, sir. Even this DC converted plot has more than a couple of banks willing to fund the loans."

"Hmm...what about the extent of the loan?"

"Meaning?"

"I mean, what is the maximum percentage of loan that we can avail on this one?"

"As I mentioned sir, still many people have a soft corner for BMRDA sites. Thus the banks are willing to go to a higher percentage, which is anywhere between seventy to eighty percent loan. However, for the DC converted plots, the maximum you will get is fifty percent of the registered value."

"Phew...thank god! Fifty percent loan is good enough for me," I butted in.

"Raj, just hold on for a moment, will you?" I was surely irritating my father by interrupting often. He turned to Nagesh, "Fifty percent of the registered value? But tell me this Nagesh, the complete price that the promoter is quoting will be shown as the registered value, right? Meaning, we can claim fifty percent loan on the total value of the property that is being quoted?"

"Hmm...that's a good question sir. Let me call up the promoter right away and get it clarified."

While Nagesh was trying to dial the number, I went to my father, "Dad, you are needlessly getting hassled. They will give fifty percent loan, right? What is the issue?"

"Raj, don't behave like a small child." My father had a more serious tone in his voice, so I stopped fooling around. "Do you know what it means when the registered value is lesser than the final value that you have to pay?"

I tried to focus on understanding what my father was saying, "Sorry no, tell me Dad." I waited attentively.

"Let me give you an example. Let's say that the developer has told you that a particular plot will cost you a hundred rupees. But the value that will be shown on papers, that is, the value that will be shown to the government will be, let's say, eighty rupees. This eighty rupees in this example is the registration value. For all legal purposes, eighty will be used as the reference point. Which means, your loan eligibility of fifty percent will not be on the actual value of rupees hundred, it will be on eighty. Do you understand?"

"Eh...ok...I did understand. But the difference between the two...I mean rupees twenty, will be paid by whom?"

"Your father."

"What?"

"You will have to pay it from your pocket in hard cash Raj. It will not be accounted for anywhere. In layman's terms, it is black money for the developer. Do you get it?"

"Woah! That is a big issue then."

"Yes, it is. For salaried people like you and me, it will make sense when hundred percent of the value is considered as registered value. Any lesser than this will be a nightmare for you."

Nagesh returned to us after finishing with his phone call. "So I checked with the developer. You are right, sir. They are not quoting hundred percent of the value that you need to pay as the registration value. It will be seventy percent of the total amount."

"Then Nagesh..." I tried to do some mental math, "You mean that if the value of the land is rupees hundred, I need to pay off rupees thirty from my own pocket in cash to the developer. Then again, in the remainder of the rupees seventy that I owe to them, as this is a DC converted site, I will get only rupees thirty-five as the loan amount?"

"That's correct," he admitted.

"Is it the same in the other two plots you showed us, Nagesh?" asked my father.

"I will check that, sir. But I am sure that most of them in these regions will surely have some amount that you need to pay to them over and above the registration value," concluded Nagesh.

"I think we will have an issue then to proceed with these, Nagesh," Dad again said what I intended to.

"No, I understood that, sir. It is my mistake. I should not have assumed that this part won't be an issue. I should have considered this point as well while choosing the plots to show you." He was indeed feeling bad.

"Hey, that is not your fault man," I tried to tell him.

"Yes Nagesh. I get what you say. That is how the business on land works, I guess. Developers will play this card to make more unaccounted profits. But how will people like us get the amount to pay in black is a bigger question," my father said, and both of us could feel the sorrow in my father's voice.

Nagesh didn't want us to give up hope. "Don't worry, sir. I will check with some of my contacts again. There will surely be some plots where there will be no black money business. I will let you know those as soon as I find out," he promised.

Both I and my father assured Nagesh that we were extremely thankful to him for having taken so much trouble for us, and parted way with him repeating that he would let us know once he found out about the plots where we could invest.

"What Dad? This is becoming an onion business," I told my father as we walked to my bike.

"It is becoming unreasonably costlier and unpredictable by the day, you mean?"

"No Dad. It is like peeling an onion. You keep peeling each layer thinking you will get to the end of it. It will make your eyes tearful during the process, and in the end you realise after you have peeled all layers, that there actually was nothing in it!"

"Ha ha!" My father liked the metaphor. I did remember that my behaviour while addressing the land he had bought was quite rude. In fact, had he not asked the right questions, I would have hastily ended up signing for something outrageous.

"I am sorry Dad."

"Hmm..."

"I am really sorry. I got carried away too much."

"That's natural son. Don't get worked up."

"Thank you Dad."

"But promise me one thing, Raj."

"What is that, Dad?"

"You still have a long way to go in your life. There will be many such decisions that will come your way, having the capacity to change the course of your life in a big way. Never take decisions without thinking out all possible angles. Also, when you think you are done making your decision, that is the most important point in time when you will not give out your decision. Mull over it or sleep over it. If you still believe it is right, only then go ahead."

I didn't see this coming through, but I kind of didn't miss that I got goose-bumps for a bit as I agreed with the well said words from my father.

After our slow and measured walk came to an end, and we reached the bike, I asked my father, "Can we not miss the wedding Dad?"

"No, we need to go. What will Byrappa think about me? That we just came here, took his right hand man's help in seeing the plots and went away without attending his daughter's wedding? That will be unacceptable."

"Oh come on Dad, you anyway show your face to him one or twice in a decade."

"What?"

"I am just kidding Dad. Come, I will take you to Byrappa Uncle's daughter's wedding."

"We should also take some flowers. I have come only with cash as the gift. It will be nice if we go there with a bouquet."

"But tell me Dad, do you think that Byrappa Uncle would have gifted me a piece of land if I had married his daughter Mangala from Nelamangala?"

"I don't know if he would have parted with one of his plots or not, but I would have surely parted from you for encouraging dowry."

"Oh Dad, why do you get so serious in life? Come, let me get your flowers."

"What? Why will you get me flowers? I am not your girlfriend."

"Your son doesn't have a girlfriend, Dad."

"Don't worry. There is Valentine's Day coming up. Find a good girl and propose to her."

"Why not? Do you know any florists around?"

"I keep visiting Nelamangala every fortnight to block plots, isn't it? I will know all the florists in the town," he laughed at his own joke.

Speaking of florists and Valentine's Day reminded me of the previous year. Ladies reading this might hate me more than they already had decided to, when they see that I am bad at being a valentine. I suck at gifting, and perhaps only someone like Sandhya could tolerate me for some time. But last Valentine's Day, I thought I would surprise her by gifting her flowers, which I knew she would have least expected from me.

We were to meet near the Forum in Koramangala, and thought we would catch a movie and have lunch together. I observed that she hadn't expected me to meet up for a movie and have lunch, and was pleasantly surprised. Now I was proud of myself that I was going to further exceed her expectations by getting her flowers.

As planned, I reached an hour earlier than I was supposed to, and had blindly guessed that there ought to be some or the other good florist in that area. As I walked in search of it, I did come across a couple of florists on the road-side. I intentionally avoided them. As this was pretty much the first time I was getting her flowers, though we were seeing each other for some time now, I wanted it to look at least a bit decent. In the gullies of Koramangala, I finally found a well-maintained florist shop.

I entered and knew that I had come to the right place. The way the flowers were decorated, and put in select containers in an orderly manner, gave me the sense that this was the right shop.

There was no customer around at that hour, which to me was a surprise considering it was Valentine's Day. Maybe they had come earlier in the day or maybe they will come in the evening to buy flowers, I told myself. A lady approached me from the counter with a glad smile, “May I help you, sir?”

“Yes please. I need to buy flowers for my girlfriend.”

“Sure sir. Have you taken a look at our range of flowers displayed here, sir?”

“Yes, they all look great. Can you suggest something for me then?” I asked.

“I will sir, but tell me do you know the history of Valentine’s Day?”

“Eh... No, sorry. I wasn’t very attentive in my History classes,” I laughed. But she didn’t. The joke went clearly over her head. I continued, “Of course I know about St. Valentine, Ma’am”

“Oh okay, then we will get to choosing the bouquet for you,” she said, thankfully coming to the point.

“Yup, sure.”

“So do you want just one variety of flowers sir, or do you want to mix it up a little?”

“Hmm...I like the idea of mixing up a little.”

“Great sir, so as you can see, we have put the variety on display. Lilies, carnations, tulips, iris, tuberoses, hyacinths and a few more that are imported. Which one do you want to choose, sir?”

“Ahem...you will have to go a bit slow on that ma’am. What are the flowers you mentioned?” Damn! I thought, I didn’t seem to register any other flowers apart from lilies. Too many questions popped up in my head. Where did the brilliant roses go? And what are these new breeds of flowers coming in and confusing poor men like me? Also, she didn’t say anything about violets. All my college life there were jokes I’ve heard starting with ‘roses are red, violets are blue’. Then again, I got further confused at the joke itself, “Wait a moment,” I told myself, “Violets are blue in colour? Aren’t they supposed to be violet? I mean violet is a colour right?” I thought about VIBGYOR, and then was sure there was this colour violet. Seemed like both the flower and the colour violet had joined the extinct list.

"Sorry sir, my mistake. I meant, we have carnations here," she showed a place where some eight varieties of flowers were placed and I couldn't get which one she was showing.

"Carnations, as in like reincarnations?" I asked her without thinking much.

"Excuse me sir?" she was evidently not happy with my response. She continued, "Then you have hyacinths," she said.

"Like Cynthia spelt in reverse?" I asked her, again she was offended. I mean, come on dude! I am not an expert in flowers.

"And then there are tuberoses," she said. I swear this time I was not going to open my mouth, but she for some reason anticipated that I would do that and said, "Not tuberculosis, sir."

Not bad, she was getting the drift. I hadn't thought of that at all. "Listen Ma'am. I am sorry. I don't know a lot about flowers. Can you just help me with the assortment for this bouquet please? I don't want to keep my girlfriend waiting, if you know what I mean?" I said in the nicest possible way.

"Of course sir," she smiled and accepted.

"Thank you," I looked at my watch, hoping it would be done soon.

She sat amongst the spread of flowers, "So I will use some chrysanthemums, sir?" she asked me.

"But you didn't mention that in the initial list of the flowers," I noted.

She raised her eyebrows and responded, "Very observant sir." That made me smile, while she picked up a few chrysanthemums and added to the bouquet.

"What about lilies, sir?" she asked.

"Lilies would be just fine," I winked both my eyes affirming my point.

"We have Himalayan lily and Calla lily. Which one do you prefer, sir?"

Shoot! Now you've started having varieties of lilies as well to make men's job more difficult? I didn't have a clue how each of those silly lilies looked like, so I just said, "The one at the left," nodding my head in a knowing a manner.

"Oh, Calla? Good choice sir." I gave a mock salute. Yeah, what else? I was running out of new expressions.

"Shall I go with some hyacinths, sir?" She asked.

"What about daffodils? You never mentioned them."

"Oh! That's correct." There was an expression on her face of being caught while stealing flowers from the neighbourhood uncle's house.

I had been straining my brain to remember the name of the poem I was forced to by-heart and recite in an oral test by my English teacher in the school. After a lot of brain racking I remembered it was 'Daffodils'. There was no way I wouldn't use it to scare this lady off, so finally, after decades of reciting the poem in front of a large audience, today it came in for some practical use in my life.

"I am sorry, sir, the stock of daffodils is yet to come today."

"Never mind, let's go with some tulips and carnations," I said with authority. This was easy man! If I could pick these names up in less than half an hour, I am sure any guy in the world can.

She was finally done with the bouquet, and it looked quite grand, thanks to all the right choices I had made. I paid the lady, which I found a little expensive, but realised there were a few imported flowers she'd used as well, and she'd arranged the bouquet in a pretty basket.

I managed to reach the place of meeting on time. Sandhya looked as elegant as ever, a wide smile completing her attire. She was thrilled at the bouquet I had got for her, which made me feel that the whole effort was totally worth it.

"I didn't know you could be so romantic Raj." She was very happy.

"I too didn't know," I said honestly, but figured that it was not necessarily the right response at the time. But it was Sandhya after all, and she understood me quite well.

"Looks grand, where did you get this from and how much did it cost?"

Here's where guys, you need to be careful and use your judgement in answering as the situation demands. I know it because I didn't do it in this case. "Yeah, it cost six hundred and fifty bucks," I said casually, moving towards the counter to buy movie tickets.

"What!"

"Hmm...?"

"Raj you paid six hundred and fifty rupees for these flowers?"

"Yeah, why?"

"It is so costly! Why would you spend so much on flowers?"

"Costly, is it? How much would have been the right amount?"

She looked a bit sad. "We could have had a good lunch or watched a movie with that money."

I didn't know what to say.

She realised it quickly that my intentions were right, and said, "Look, I am sorry. I mean, this is really sweet of you to get me flowers. Come, let's go watch a movie."

This made me feel better, as we moved into the multiplex.

"You know what?" she asked as we entered the movie hall.

"What Sandhya?"

"It would have been perfect, if there were roses in the bouquet as well," and occupied a seat.

I just realised there were no walls available in immediate proximity to go bang my head on.

"There there, I think that guy has flowers," said my Dad, and I pulled the bike over.

We had had enough time on our hands, so we had taken our own time to travel slowly, trying to locate any florists on the way. As we had anticipated, we found one near the wedding hall.

I asked my Dad to stay outside as I would get a bouquet quickly.

"Welcome sir, how can I help you?" said the lady inside the shop.

"Hey! I just need a bouquet to gift at a wedding."

"Of course sir. Would you like to see our assortment of flowers?"

"Sorry?"

"We have daffodils, carnations, lilies..."

"Please stop it right there," I held up my hand. I understand I do hold up my hand often at times, but such situations demand that too.

The lady was a bit perplexed thinking she'd said something wrong. "I am sorry, sir?" She looked at me questioningly.

"Firstly, please tell me if you have a branch in Koramangala area, in Bangalore?"

"Huh...no sir. This is the only shop I have."

"Oh okay." I was a bit comforted. Maybe it's the job. They just sound all the same, the way we folks from BPO kind of have the same way of talking and doing things; modus operandi, I think it is called.

"So sir, I was saying, do you want to look at an assorted bouquet? I can help you with the same," she offered.

Again, this was a hand-holding-high moment, but it would be too much repetition if I do it in quick succession. "No ma'am, not at all. Even in chocolates and donuts, I avoid assortments nowadays."

"Sir?" She couldn't follow.

"Just roses will do please," I said and returned to my father with the bouquet of flowers.

"That was quick Raj," opined my Dad.

"Yes, Dad. I'd learnt it the hard way."

"What? I didn't understand."

"Nothing Dad, let's get in to the wedding hall. I am beginning to feel hungry already."

I observed that the marriage hall looked quite small from the outside. Only when we entered did I realise that it was indeed much smaller than I had imagined.

My father surely had the same opinion, as he was trying to locate a seat. "Looks like this hall has a capacity of only a hundred and fifty folks."

"And I think looking at the crowd, at least twelve hundred have been invited," I concluded.

"This is quite crowded, Raj. I think instead of waiting for a seat, we should go ahead and give the bouquet to the couple."

"That's a good idea Dad. I think the ceremony has just concluded and I see the couple accepting gifts on the dais."

We didn't have to go in search of the queue, as the ultra long queue was visible right in front of us. We tried and joined in, which in itself was an effort.

"Dad! This queue resembles the one you have at Tirupati, doesn't it?"

My father shook his head and commented, "There is a difference son. You get laddoos at the end in Tirupati."

"When my wedding takes place Dad, let's please not book any marriage halls or invite thousands this way."

"I was thinking of something else."

"What's that?"

"I was just imagining the way we have been joking since yesterday, if you were to be the groom for Mangala, this would have been your wedding right now."

"Dad!" I looked around, hoping none had heard.

"It's okay Raj, no one has any time to listen to us."

"Byrappa Uncle must be a big name in this town. Half of Nelamangala is here, I think."

"You are forgetting something."

"What now?"

"Not just people from Nelamangala, even people like you and me have come all the way from Bangalore."

"Ah, like that."

"Even I am feeling hungry now," said my father.

"We should have got something parcelled from either Mr Maiya or Mr Maani's," I said as I observed that while we were waiting our turn in the queue, there was a good set of population joining the married couple from the other side.

I can understand if there is someone very old who cannot stand in the queue for long, but every other joker present on the other side wanted to finish off posing for a photo with the married couple, and started to make another queue. If that was not good enough, the people standing in our own queue gently nudged past through us, as if it were a national highway and they were overtaking a slow moving vehicle.

It is only of late that I have made an effort to tell those morons overtaking others in a queue to get behind, as I used to consider such conversations avoidable earlier. Though I would have liked to tell those idiots who went past us, after all it was someone's wedding and I didn't want to be a reason for any argument taking place.

I didn't understand the desperation that some of them showed to get even further from the queue and reach the couple. Or maybe I was being harsh to judge them. It was quite possible that the moron who'd just passed me a few minutes ago, pushing others on the way like a raging bull, had a train to catch to Nagaland immediately after the wedding.

There were a couple of college boys with their bags on and shirt buttons undone with the collars held up. Whenever they spoke, which was most of the time, I saw them talking at an intolerable decibel level. Every fourth word, I counted, was an expletive, which was subconsciously used by them so that people could take them seriously and be afraid of them. The 'I don't care' attitude shouted out that they do care a lot about what others perceive them to be. Looks and attitude aside, even these two had sneaked ahead of us slyly, and were waiting for an opportunity for the gentleman ahead to just relax for a moment, so that they could duck and get ahead of him. The poor rascals perhaps had an important exam to attend immediately after meeting this married couple.

As there was enough and more time for us to reach the other end of this tunnel of a queue, I did spare a thought to those sneaking and creating another queue on the other side of the hall. The writing was on the wall that there was a rebellion coming, and these jokers who were busy trying to create a parallel queue, were the chief members of such a rebellion.

One of the ladies who seemed to be of my age had been standing behind me in the queue some time ago and now had joined the rebels. These people had all the qualities of becoming politicians –

not leaders, mind you – as jumping from one party to another and sneaking ahead when others are not looking were obviously the most prominent qualities needed in that last resort of scoundrels. This lady, poor thing, had all the right I would say, to jump the queue and leave at the earliest. Don't we average people have any common sense to know that she'd perhaps spent a lot of time and money getting herself ready for the wedding, though it is someone else's? If she stands in the queue with bloody mortals like us, won't all that make-up wear off? How do we think will then she appear in the photographs that were being taken as she would stand alongside the bride? Of course she must have been one of the closest cousins of Mangala or maybe her best friend, to have tried to jump the queue. It is surely not for us to argue why she wasn't behind the scenes instead, trying to help out the bride during the event. So this lady, immediately after posing alongside Mangala, updating that snap on Instagram, must have had an appointment with the local tele-serial director, for a role in one of these relationship-breaking house-splitting soaps that most of us watch and encourage. If she managed to reach the auditions soon with her make-up still on, there at least will be a bleak chance of being considered for the daughter's role in that soap. She has to be late only by a few minutes, and there, her make-up would have worn down and the director would have ended up selecting her for the role of the mother. Yes, I agree, she had all the rights to jump the queue.

"Why are you looking at that lady in an offensive manner Raj? Please behave yourself, this is a wedding," said my father, irritated with my behaviour. I started to explain, but then thought my father will be more shocked if he knew what I was thinking. He then added, "But in case you want me to find out from her parents if they're open to form an alliance, though I am surprised at your choice, then I can go and talk once we are done with wishing the couple."

"Dad please! I was looking at her like that because her make-up is scary, that's all," I told my father.

The queue had taken the shape of a swarm of bees, as we were almost carried towards our goal. Surprised at the sudden increase in movement of the queue, I tried to peek to see what the cause was, and then I saw Nagesh there! The hero's entry had happened in the movie and all villains had to take a back-seat. He put brakes on the rebellious queue, which now had the only choice to come join our queue, he also nominated some more people around the married couple to collect the gifts, and started pushing more people to pose per photo instead of very small groups taking their own sweet time.

I saw the heavy make-up lady now passing by us to go stand at the beginning of the queue, and was all smiles with the cheap thrills my heart found to be so much fun. My father looked at me, and said, "I can talk to her parents Raj. You can be open with me."

"Oh god Dad! Why are you hell-bent on getting me married? I don't like her, trust me please."

"Okay, if you say so."

Then it was the transformation that I saw in the colourful and collar-full college kids. The collars had immediately come down, with even the top-most shirt button put in place. They were surely regretting not having a tie and a tie-pin that they wanted to be seen with when they'd come in front of Nagesh. I fast-forwarded some years and could see me casting my vote to Nagesh when he would contest for the chief minister's post.

This efficiency from him brought us to the couple in quick time. To keep up with the spirit, we too rushed to wish the couple and parted with the bouquet. I posed along with my Dad, smiled acknowledging at Nagesh and we were off the dais.

"Woah, finally! I thought we would be stuck in the queue like we are usually stuck in the Silk-board signal in Bangalore for hours."

"Good god, thanks to Nagesh. I like that chap. I think he has a bright future. Let's quickly leave now and reach Bangalore. I am very tired."

"No Dad, what are you saying?"

"It's irritating to be around for any more time Raj. Let's go."

"We have both been hungry for quite some time and we have come to a wedding, Dad. Let's please have lunch and then leave."

"You never know how much time it will take. We will have something on the way in some restaurant."

"Come on! I am sure it will not take too much time. Let's quickly eat and leave," I almost pleaded, pushed by furious hunger pangs.

My father gave in after a while, and we both walked towards the dining hall. There was just one entrance in and out of the dining hall. I had to hold my father's hand so that we didn't lose each other in this wave of people. A few more steps, and I knew my dad was right. We should have left the place to eat elsewhere. I looked back to see that we were at the point of no return, so we had to go in.

All the seats were occupied and lunch was just being served. The coordinator asked us to stand next to others who were to start eating, and then occupy their place once they were done. This surely was a never before experience as we waited for the others to start their lunch standing next to them.

Trying not to embarrass the folks seated, I and my father started to look at the ceiling and chatted away some nonsense. The folks who had to serve had a tough time as they tried to manoeuvre in the cramped place. There were instances when those folks took advantage of me standing next to the guests, and I was asked to pass a few bananas once and ice cream in the second instance. Both instances, I expected that the guests having lunch might say that they don't want the bananas or the ice cream so that I could gobble them up, but they happily took them from me, and also were shameless enough not to thank me.

My father's favourite candidate for daughter-in-law walked into the dining hall, and like us, stood next to few others who were busy finishing their meals. Even before dad could suggest anything, I called him, showed her, and said, "Don't ask again Dad. I am not interested."

But then my father had already gotten into the groove. So once he said, "Raj, two o'clock, now."

I looked at the watch, and corrected him, "No Dad, it's still just one o'clock. I know it feels like two, considering how hungry and exhausted we are, but that's not the case."

"Stupid fellow. Look at that side, at two o'clock." I followed the finger he was pointing to, and saw a lady seated, busy eating.

"What is it, Dad?"

"How do you find her? I think she is sitting with her parents on the right. If you want to, I can go speak to them to find out more."

"Dad, please look at the left side as well. Her husband is present with her. You want to go speak to him?"

"Oh, nonsense. Is he her husband…really? Okay fine, seems like. So let's drop it," he concluded, or so I thought.

"Raj, eight o'clock," he said.

"Dad are you checking out girls in the dining hall?"

"Shut up and just look at eight o'clock."

I turned at a certain angle and saw that there were some elderly ladies seated, who were way beyond my age. I was a little disappointed that my father thought I was in such a hurry to get married, and was suggesting some senior folks.

"Why are you looking at four o'clock, idiot fellow? I said eight o'clock."

"Oh come on Dad! I don't understand this clock thing."

"What are you saying? Is it because you use a digital watch?"

"No Dad, I just don't understand the angle we are supposed to look at, and what should be the reference."

"Okay fine, just look there." He pointed his finger to another lady, surely not elder to me, and asked my opinion.

"Dad, I know it is quite boring to stand next to people when they are eating, but I don't think checking out people in the vicinity is the right way to kill time."

"Just answer me. How do you find her? Should I approach her parents?"

"Dad, she is good looking, but I don't know her. Can we not do it some other time please?"

That is when the lady's kid came running to her, and my father was awarded with a Santoor soap moment.

Thankfully my Dad didn't have to shortlist more girls for me, as the seats were vacated and we finally sat down for lunch. It was the turn for other folks to stand beside us and watch us eat.

Soon we were done, and my father, wanting to have areca nut and betel leaf, joined other elders in the corner at a table, and thankfully the traffic was bearable. I informed my father that I would stay outside the entrance to get some fresh air, and waited for him.

I peeked in after a few minutes when I didn't see him return. He was engaged in conversation with a man whom I hadn't seen before. I guessed it must be a common friend who knew Byrappa Uncle and my father. So I remained outside, waiting for him to return.

Once my father was with me, I announced, "I will want to rest once we reach home, Dad. It's been quite an adventure today."

"Yes, before that Raj. You saw that I was talking to that man?"

"Yes, I did."

"So he is Revathi's father."

"Who is Revathi?"

"No no, let me complete. So he wanted to find out if we are interested in a marriage alliance."

"Eh...weird. Just like you, all fathers are keen to find out matches for their kids in such weddings, I presume."

"Nothing like that. But I have taken his contact details. There is no hurry or pressure for you to respond. We can talk about it later."

"But is the girl present here? We could have seen her, right?" I said, and my father was taken aback.

"Oh, ok. I didn't expect you to say that. And I mean it in a good way."

"Yeah, I understand Dad. We can at least know who that Revathi girl is, and later on let her father know."

"So she's seen you and was interested in the alliance it seems."

"Wow that was quick. Let me see her picture. Do you have a snap or did he message it to you on your phone?"

"No, but you know that girl. It's the same one whose make-up you kept commenting about."

"Dad!"

After I realised that the Nelamangala land was practically out of my reach, I let my father know that it was time for us to look into the advertisements in the paper cut-outs.

On one of the weekdays, he came down to my place. He reached out to his hand bag to pull out a file in which he had neatly maintained all the cut-outs.

"Let me see. There's something in Sarjapur Road, I see."

"Yes, that's correct. I hear that most of your IT-ITeS companies are growing in that region, and many from this industry seem to be investing in that area. So I thought you should begin with that first."

"Hmm... Nice. Cost-wise, it does not seem too high or too low. Also, you are right in saying that all IT-ITeS crowd is jam-packed there. I will go check this out."

"I will come with you as well," he offered.

"No Dad. You have been travelling a lot already, and remember we have to go to Mysore this weekend to collect our money? I surely will need you for that one. I will go to this Sarjapur Road plot by myself."

▲

The next day I spent some time with the team explaining what needed to be done in my absence, as I had been doing for a few weeks now, and they seemed to understand and execute it quite well. Thus, I also realised that irrespective of me staying late or leaving on time, work was getting completed. I smiled to myself for having learnt this lesson a bit late in my career. I left office much earlier and tried to reach the stipulated location.

I called up the number given in the advertisement. My father had already called them up, and it seemed the route shouldn't be a problem. I just wanted to keep them informed that I was on the way and confirm there would be someone present to take me through the property.

"Hello, Prima locations office, may I know who's speaking?" said the voice from the other side.

"Hi, I am Raj. We had called up during the weekend to enquire about a plot of land in Sarjapur Road."

"Look sir, there are many who call us to know the details of Prima Locations. Please tell me your details, and I will see how I can help," said the voice in a matter of fact tone, with a strong local accent.

It was my mistake. I knew that I hadn't even introduce myself, and hence I did that and also informed them about my father calling them.

"Oh! Mr Setty's son you are? Very respectable fellow, your father. Even if you are fifty percent like him in your life, you will succeed."

"Excuse me?"

"So you wanted the exact location for Prima. Look sir, it is at prime location only. But I will also tell you that the prices are non-negotiable."

"Sure buddy, but let me at least come and have a look at the property."

"That is right. But I just didn't want simple confusions to exist leading to complications," he added.

I figured out that he liked to hear his own voice and English, and hence would continue to go on this way. "I am at the traffic signal. Can you tell me any landmark please?"

"No sir, no landmark. Only Prima."

"Dude, what are you saying?"

"Landmark constructions is not us. They have another project and they are our competitors. We are Prima, one and only."

"Yes, got it. I didn't mean any Landmark constructions man. I meant to say, how do I come to Prima?"

"From where you will come?"

"I work at Electronic City."

"Oh! That is like very near."

"Yes, it is not far from Sarjapur Road. So how do I come?"

"By bus, it will be forty-five minutes, and by car it will be thirty-five minutes."

I was irritated with this idiot by now, "And by bike?"

"If you ride on footpath and come, then twenty-five minutes." He didn't even get the sarcasm.

"Dude listen, I need to talk to someone else. Can you hand over the phone to your manager?"

"Oh no sir. I am the manager."

"Yeah, and I am Ambani."

"No, no. It is not a bad joke. My workers have gone and joined Landmark Constructions yesterday. I am still to hire people. So as of now, I am only taking all the calls," he explained laboriously.

"Ah okay! No sir listen. I want to come to your office, or go to your project site. I am travelling on my bike. I need to know the route to reach the place."

"One problem is at least solved."

"And what's that?"

"The office location and the property location are one and the same. So you need not run around searching for it."

"Okay fine, now can you tell me where do I come? The route to your place, I mean."

"So you know this Piwro office in Sarjapur Road?"

"Yes, I do. It's quite easy to get there."

"Correct, it is very near to Prima Locations."

"Okay great. I will reach there in thirty minutes, and then I will call you."

As this was before the evening's peak hour, I reached quite soon, and called up the Prima locations' manager.

"You reached very fast."

"Yes, there wasn't much traffic. So what's the way from here? Is there any landmark? And by landmark, I mean any famous place? Like a mall, theatre, temple, or anything like that?"

"Beer shop."

"What?"

"You will get a beer shop on the way."

"Okay, fine. Which direction?"

"So you are Piwro office!"

"What are you saying sir?"

"No, wait. Think like that for a minute. You are Piwro office campus. So you need to come to your left side till you find the beer shop in the service road."

"Sure, but any idea what is the distance? Like is it a kilometre or less?"

"In Bangalore, distance is relative, and relatives are at a distance."

No, I didn't react to this. Otherwise, I think this guy would assume it as encouragement. I kept mum.

"So you don't know the distance?"

"Not very sure sir. But don't miss the beer shop."

"Or at least can you tell me if it is very near from Piwro or far?"

He thought for a good minute and said, "Medium."

"At least, do you know the name of the beer shop?"

"Tirumala bar."

"Half the bars in Bangalore are named that way, mister. How will I search?"

"Trust in Tirumala, and come off."

"Really? Aren't there any more famous places that you know?"

"Sir, there is no other Tirumala bar in that road, and it is quite famous. Trust me, I tried searching for a bar in that road one day and located this in the end. In fact, if you want to take a break, I suggest you go there and come. The owner knows me now. You can take my name..."

"Okay boss, I will come. Let me call you when I get to Tirumala bar. You said it will be to my left?"

"Correct, and one more thing," he said before I was going to hang up.

"Tell me."

"You wouldn't be comfortable getting something parcelled for me?"

"Parcelled, from here?"

"Yeah from Tirumala bar."

Again, silence, I learnt over the past few months, is the best response to some questions.

"Okay, I understand you don't want to do it. No problem. My interview candidate is coming after an hour. I will ask him to get it. See you in some time." He hung up.

The number of times I curse people who don't follow lane discipline or are riding/driving badly is many. But I was getting to know how it was to be at the receiving end. Both the main road and the service lanes were getting packed now with the peak hour traffic approaching, and I still had no choice but to go slow in search of Tirumala bar.

I had surely come more than a couple of kilometres and there was no Tirumala bar anywhere. In fact, I was over cautious and asked a couple of small time bars around, but neither of them was Tirumala bar.

The honking behind me was highly irritating, and it obviously gets to you after a point in time. So I thought it was better to stop the vehicle and walk pushing it. While it was more of a strain for me this way, at least the incessant honking had stopped and people weren't cursing or abusing me under their breath. Now, I was a harmless and helpless guy whose bike wasn't starting.

I did this with a basic expectation that the bar should just be round the corner, but that corner was conning me and I was not able to get there at all.

Meanwhile I got a call. In such a situation, even the smallest of things can irritate you to a great extent. I just stopped, and took a deep breath, and letting the weight of the bike fall on my thigh, I took Dad's call.

"Yes, Dad. Make it quick."

"Where are you Raj? Did you go to that Prima Locations?"

"Not yet Dad."

"You seem to be tired and breathing heavily. What happened?"

"I will speak in detail once I get home, Dad."

"Okay, no problem. Where are you now?"

"I am trying to find where on earth this Tirumala bar is..."

There was silence from my Dad, and he said in a low deliberate tone, "Listen son, I know the last few months have been harsh on you. But trust me, drinking is not the solution to your problems."

"Oh dear god Dad, No!"

"Okay, what?"

"Why would I go to Tirumala bar in daylight, that too seeking permission from my office, Dad? It is a bloody landmark that Prima Locations' manager has given me. That's why I am searching for it."

"Ah! Like that? Okay then you carry on. May Lord Tirumala be with you."

I had walked on feet for nearly a kilometre now, and still there was no Tirumala bar. Though good with directions, I was just a bit worried in case I had missed the landmark. Hence, when I reached a place from where I could locate a big mall, I decided to call the manager again to verify."

"Ah yes yes, just after that mall, you will find Tirumala bar."

"Just after, is it?"

"Yes Mr Raj, just after that mall, you travel some distance and it is right there to your left."

"So is it like the same distance you made me travel from Piwro till here, or even further?"

"What Mr Raj, now you are pulling my leg."

"I don't know about your leg sir, but mine are aching badly."

"Why, I thought you are coming in bike," he said, but I surely didn't have the patience to explain.

"I will come there and tell you." And I hung up.

There was no way I could have continued to walk, so I decided to ride slowly. It was five in the evening, and I knew there was no way I could avoid the evening rush.

Again, I had travelled some distance with no luck. I am a stout agnostic, but had I been a believer and searched and pained myself so much, I am sure even Lord Tirumala would have transpired in front of me, and yet this bar would not show itself.

I saw a bunch of college kids approaching from the opposite direction. I thought it was better to check with them before I get lost. "Hey boss, Hi!"

"Yes?" spoke one of them diligently.

"Can you tell me where Tirumala bar is?" And by the time I had ended the sentence, I realised it was a mistake, and I shouldn't have asked him.

He and his friends gave me almost a dressing down look. While I didn't own a Harley Davidson bike, mine was no worse, and I wore a Harley Davidson jacket to compensate for it. Then, my Ray Ban glasses; original, mind you. Not those that you get in Commercial Street for 1/10th the price. And then the branded boots. Once they were done scanning, those young minds had a tough equation to solve, for which they were not able to find the answer.

"So guys, are you unable to understand why I am asking the details of Tirumala bar or is it that you actually don't know?"

Stunned silence and shock in their wide eyes. I realised there was no use scandalising them further, and just put up my hand and said, "That's completely fine, folks. It is okay...Happens to all of us."

And I left the group. If these kids didn't know where Tirumala bar was, maybe the future of the nation was in the right hands, I consoled myself.

Little did I realise that behind this group of school guys, there was a girl's group of the same school, and seeing me depart without an answer they assumed I would approach them next, and readily offered, "Yes sir. How can we help you?"

Lightening, they say, does not strike the same place twice. I just smiled and nodded my head as genuinely as possible. There was no way I would ask these kids about 'that-which-shouldn't-be-named'.

I had hardly ridden few metres, when I saw a decent looking man approaching from the other direction with an opaque cover in his right hand, looking around with guilt spilling from his being.

I stopped the bike right in front of him, scaring the wits out of him. His lips started to chant some mantras. There couldn't be anything else in that black cover than a product that was sold from the holy Tirumala bar.

"Wha...what?" he asked me.

"Sir please. Wait. Just tell me where Tirumala bar is."

He turned and pointed to a corner shop, which was hardly 8x10 feet in size. If I had blinked, I would have missed it.

"Thank you so much sir." My heart went out for such decent looking people who walk around buying alcohol in black opaque covers.

"Don't mention." He tried to hurry past me.

"Wait, sir."

"What?"

"Should I get you another bottle of your favourite?" I offered with a wink, which I don't know why he seemed to misunderstand, and jogged away chanting the same mantra.

I called up Prima Locations again and spoke, "Project Tirumala bar over and out."

He clearly didn't understand even a bit, and asked me to repeat myself.

"Sir I have reached the bar. Which direction should I take to reach your place?"

"Ah good, good. So you see there is a left turn immediately after the bar."

"Right."

"No, I said left."

"Yes, I meant correct. I got it. So after taking the left, what next?"

"You will need to travel straight for some time till you find a tea stall."

"Oh ho! Which tea stall is it?"

"It is Kaka tea stall"

"What?"

He spelt it for me, "K..a..k..a…Kaka tea stall."

"Sir, are you kidding me?"

"What? No, I won't ask you to get a cup of tea for me. Don't worry. Come soon."

"And you won't know the distance from the bar till the Kaka tea stall?"

"No, but it is not very far. Just keep coming as the road takes you. You just come on your bike quickly. There is still sunlight, and we can visit the property soon."

I took a deep breath and started off again.

He called me up immediately, "Listen Mr Raj. You will get a 'Y' junction after traveling for a few minutes. Take the leftish route."

"Okay, I will do that."

I'd observed how the density of population reduced as I left the bar. It was just a mud road, but had several deviations. My bike seemed to complain for what I was making it go through. A couple of times the bike's footrest bumped into heavy rocks. I knew by now that when that Prima guy says few minutes, it meant at least ten minutes.

Then it was a village, whose narrow lanes I passed through, and took a small break there to check if I was on the right track. I saw an old man selling tender coconuts. "Sir, good evening. Can you tell me where Prima Locations is?"

He just shook his head.

"Or would you know where Kaka tea stall is?" He seemed offended with the question for he knitted his brows.

I thought I should ask someone else further down the lane. But then the old man spoke, "I don't know about Kaka tea shop, but keep going on this route for half a mile and at the end of this village, there is one tea stall at the left. You might take five minutes to reach there. The roads aren't good, I am warning you."

I mean, this is it, right? Such are the people we need for a better India. What precision and what no non-sense attitude man! How well he told me the distance, and the time and that the roads were bad. If such people are sitting in a village selling tender coconuts, and people like this Prima manager are selling properties and making crores of rupees, it forces us to think where the nation is headed.

Here, I was trying to buy a plot in Sarjapur Road, but surely I had reached the Sarjapur town. It was like travelling the whole way to Mysore to have Mysore Pak.

The old tender coconut guy was absolutely right. We should have such people sitting and designing GPS instead of relying on satellites. I reached there in around five minutes, and there was a tea stall at the corner at the precise location that was indicated to me. God bless his soul, I prayed for him. I took my cell phone to call up Prima Locations, but then thought I deserve a cup of tea from Kaka tea stall. I went to the vendor and asked him, "What's up, Kaka?" I said in a light hearted manner.

He didn't stare me down the way many have already done during my journey till here, but casually asked me, "Sorry, who do you want son?"

What grace, and what calm smile. No wonder this Kaka tea stall is supposed to me famous.

"One cup tea please, Kaka," I requested.

He made it and served to me in no time. It had the perfect flavour, right amount of milk and sugar. Something I surely know the author would have appreciated. But for now, let us leave him to have tea made by himself and tell Kaka how the tea was.

"This is extremely well made Kaka, thank you."

"Not at all. You are new in these parts of the village?" he asked.

"Yes Kaka, never been in these parts. I am on my way to Prima Locations, an upcoming township. Your tea stall was given as the landmark. It should be close from here." I finished having my cup of tea and paid after thanking him.

I then got my phone to call this guy to ask him to step out of his office to locate him, but Kaka called me.

"Sorry son, if you don't mind, can I ask you something?"

"Yes surely, Kaka."

"Why are you calling me Kaka? Do I resemble any of your relatives whom you used to address with that name?"

"Sorry? No, I mean..." It slowly dawned upon me before I could speak more words. "So this is not Kaka tea stall?"

"No, it is not. Considering it is just a small time place, I haven't even named it."

"But then, even people around don't call you by that name, I take it?"

"No, no one calls me by that name. You are the first one."

"Ahem...ok, no problem. Would you by any chance know where Kaka tea stall is?"

"I hope you are not making up some names to have fun. Anyway, I don't know any tea stall by that name in this village."

I didn't wait for him to complete his sentence, as I had already dialled Prima guy's number. "Boss, I am at the only tea stall in this village, and the vendor tells me it is not Kaka tea shop."

"Oh, I know where you are. You have stopped just before Kaka tea shop's lane. Continue straight from there, and as I mentioned, come as the lane takes you, in no time, you will find the 'Y' junction and you take the left turn there. From that point onwards, Kaka tea stall is hardly one fourth of a kilometre."

I didn't pick up an argument, as I felt there was light at the end of the tunnel.

I travelled straight as he said. In a while the road deviated to the right, which I took and in the next minute I found myself parking the bike in front of a property. Having made such an error earlier, I wasn't the one to repeat it. I searched for the name of the property displayed and found it at the other end. It read 'Landmark Constructions'.

This was the same competitor the guy had spoken about. I tried looking around, but was sure there wasn't another property in the same vicinity. I shivered and shook immediately as there was a hand placed on my right shoulder. I turned around to see a guy taller to me by a good half foot, and broader than my eyes could measure, looking at me in the eye.

This guy, I am sure has acted in many Bollywood movies, where the directors desperately stereotype all south Indian rowdies. His latest flick may have been a side role in *Chennai Express*.

I was scared to the hilt. I mean, there was no habitation here, and I felt very threatened. Seeing that this guy was just giving a scary stare, I quickly thought about two options, the way I think of something when in the last moment, the month-end account reconciliation doesn't tally. The first option was to fall to his feet and ask him to take whatever he wanted from me without causing any bodily harm, and the second option was to run from there without turning back till I reach Tirumala bar; the last place where I saw some civilisation, however uncivilised they were.

Before I could make a choice, the bouncer of a guy spoke, "You are searching for someone sir?"

"Eh...Prima Locations."

"Oh super! You wanted to meet the manager?"

"Yes, but do you know him?"

"I was working there till yesterday sir. Today is my first day in Landmark Constructions. Come with me, I will show you."

"Yeah, your manager told me about it. That some of you left Prima and joined Landmark today."

I had a tough time riding doubles with him, for the vehicle hadn't experienced such a personality before. Most of the times, I used my legs to peddle my way through the bad roads.

"Strange, I don't know how I could miss it. I kept my eyes wide open in search of the 'Y' junction that I was told about. Never batted a lid, mind you."

It was hardly some way back, and he asked me to stop the bike there.

"Hey, this is where I took a right turn as there was no road ahead."

"It is right here sir," he showed.

Only then did I see there was a narrow passage which in no form of dictionary could we refer to as a road. It was not even a pathway to walk as there was thick vegetation covering it.

"Really? This is the path to go to Prima Locations?"

"Yes sir, just go straight till you find Kaka tea stall, and immediately after that..."

"I got it from here my friend. Thanks a lot for your help."

"No problem sir. Also sir, in case you don't like Prima Locations, please do come visit Landmark Constructions." He did his sales pitch.

I hadn't liked what I saw when I was there, so I would not have gone to Landmark, and I simply nodded and bid him goodbye.

There was no way I could take my bike through the narrow path. I decided to park it at the supposedly 'Y' junction, and started walking, hoping to find Kaka tea stall.

No sooner than I took some ten steps, this spot started to give me the Bandipur kind of feeling. I brushed it off and moved ahead. It was complete vegetation there and I was only guessing the path as I walked. I, in fact, was getting worried if I had crossed Karnataka border and had entered Tamil Nadu.

I was trying to jump at times to see if there was a small village on the other side where I could find the tea stall, but to no avail. If two people from Prima locations had told me the same path, there was no reason for me to think that it was wrong. But on getting into the dense vegetation, somewhere in my heart, I started to get worried. I mean, this looked like a spot where the bandit Veerappan used to visit during his Christmas vacation, when he was alive.

I had almost given up hope when I saw a very old man sitting under a tree looking up to the sky. This was some positive sign, as I hoped this was the outskirts of some village, where I will quickly find Kaka tea stall and get done with this business.

"Sir." I called the grand old man, but he continued to look at the sky. No, I didn't get scared of him, for he was blinking at times as well.

"Ain't gonna rain, grandpa," I said, knowing he wouldn't understand a thing.

Only then did he register my presence and stared at me.

"Sorry to disturb you sir, but I just want to know where the exit from this jungle is. I need to find the famous Kaka tea stall."

"Haan?" he said as he narrowed his eyes. Poor chap had issues with hearing I guessed.

I took it slow this time, "Kaka tea stall...where?" I asked him.

He seemed to remember something. Maybe it was time for him to have his diabetes tablets, so I gave him some space. He got some box from behind the tree; maybe the case where he kept all of his tablets. I didn't have water, or else I would have proudly offered it to him, for he seemed to have too many tablets to pop in.

He looked up and smiled at me, and I could see only two of his thirty-two wonders remaining, and I smiled back as well.

But then, this old man didn't seem to go beyond smiling. Oh wait! How dumb and inhuman of me? Maybe this old man had lost his ability to speak, and hence was struggling to say something. I slapped my forehead for my rude behaviour and thought I would wait for the old man to finish what he was doing so that I could apologise and then ask my way.

I looked up to see that sunlight was showing signs of fading away. I wanted to rush to Prima and back soon. I tried to lift myself with the help of one of the many branches present there to look beyond the immediate horizon, but couldn't see anything. I was clearly not looking at the right direction. Once done with my gymnastics that led to no result, I turned back to see if the old man was done with his medicine stuff.

For a moment, I could not gather what was happening. He showed me a paper cup. Maybe he wanted water or something, I just shrugged saying that I was sorry. But he wouldn't listen. When I came near to explain to him properly is when I saw that what I thought was his medicine box was actually a flask, and he showed me the paper cup and smiled, pointing his finger above, where I found a small name plate nailed on the tree beneath which the old man was seated, and the following words were written with a chalk piece, 'Kaka tea stall'.

"*Are you freaking kidding me, old man?*" I shouted, and I could hear my own echo. I tried to control my breathing.

"This is the famous Kaka tea stall that I was trying to find from that god forbidden Tirumala bar? Oh dear god!"

I called up this manager, "So Mr Raj, have you reached Kaka tea stall?" he asked.

I gritted my teeth, "Yes sir, I have. Kaka here says he wants you to come and meet him."

"Oh, is it? No worries. Let's finish off with the site visit first and then I will go meet Kaka."

"Okay...fair. Where is your office Mr Manager whose name I don't know?"

"Very near from that place. Take that narrow lane from where Kaka is sitting, and come exactly in the north-west direction for just two kilometres, and I will be standing outside the office and waving. You will not miss me for sure."

"Two...more...kilometres you say?"

"See, it might be a bit more than that. Difficult to measure, you see."

"Are you like playing some bloody prank on me?"

"Why...what happened, Mr Raj?"

"What happened? Really? This place is supposed to be on Sarjapur Road?"

"Small correction sir, it was printed as near Sarjapur Road."

"So this place is *near* Sarjapur Road?"

"Eh... Sir?"

"First of all, I think I have already entered Tamil Nadu. Now you are telling me that I need to walk for a few more kilometres to find you. Your plot is in the Western Ghats or something?"

"No Mr Raj, that is not the intention. See, compared to many other locations, this spot is still near to the Sarjapur Road."

"Yes, I get it. *Compared to Africa you mean*?" I had lost it completely by now.

"Mr Raj, I think you are a bit upset for some reason. No problem, you come tomorrow. We will sit and talk face to face. We can sort things out amicably."

"Come tomorrow? For what? To have tea in the famous Kaka tea stall? Idiot!"

"So I take it that you are not interested to apply for our project's plots then, Mr Raj?"

"What is your name?"

"Why, Mr Raj?"

"So that when I get married and if I have a boy child, I can name him after you."

"Oh, is it? It is Tirumala."

"What the f...? Your name is Tirumala?"

"Yes, why?"

"Was that your bar by any chance?"

"So I was saying Mr Raj, you don't have to be angry. I think this was just a communication gap. I sincerely apologise for any inconvenience caused." I didn't miss the fact that he avoided answering my question.

I was really done shouting at him, and didn't want to waste any further words, time or energy at him. I decided to hang up. I told him, "Next time some customer calls you expressing his or her intention to visit your project, tell them that it is some eight to ten kilometres from the main road, so that they don't go through what I had to."

"Certainly Mr Raj. I appreciate your feedback. I will make a note of it. I will also tell all the people who join my project to explain to the customer correctly and leave no confusion in the minds of the people wanting to apply for the plots."

"Thanks." I was about to hang up.

"Wait Mr Raj, one more small thing I thought I should tell you."

"Hmm..."

"So the interview candidate who was supposed to come today to join my firm didn't turn up."

I didn't know why he was updating me with all these details. I assumed he just didn't want any burnt bridges, just in case there are any future such opportunities. I didn't know how to respond. I just said "Okay."

"I remember talking to your father a few days ago, and he told me the name of the company you work for. If I am not mistaken, I think it is a call-centre. I just wanted to offer you the job of my assistant. I am sure I will pay you higher than the call-centre salary. Also no interviews for you – direct appointment. What do you think?"

"Tell me Mr Manager, have you watched the movie *Taken*?" I was expecting the answer to be in the negative.

"Yes, Mr Raj, I have watched it. Very violent movie though." He surprised me.

"So Mr Manager, I don't know who you are and I've never seen your face. If you don't apologise and cut the call immediately, I will pursue you, no matter which dense jungle you choose to hide in, I will look for you, I will find you, and I will..." the call went blank.

I went home quite late that night, and called up my father to brief him on this episode. He said something about this being Kali-Yuga, and hurled a few curses on people who put such deceiving advertisements in the papers, and told me that he will shred the remainder of such paper cut-outs that he had kept aside.

We then decided that we would just go with the flow. He also mentioned that he had received a call from Mrs Anu Nair stating that they will pay half of the amount this weekend and will need a couple of weeks' time to pay the remaining.

I thought I should close out on any pending items at office in the next few days, and went earlier than my shift timing. It turned out to be very productive, as I could finish off few key activities before the crowd got in. I had put aside the earlier day's Prima adventure and was generally in a good mood. I could spare time to sit with some new joiners and explain some critical aspects of our process and the tool that we use for the Accounts Payable work that we do.

It was nice to see some of them very keen and interested to learn and perform, and spending time this way helping them learn something gave me a sort of joy which was difficult to explain. My supervisor, whose smile I had forgotten, reminded me by sharing it a couple of times during the day. I think I realised after it had actually happened, that I had broken the pattern which I had inculcated and had become a slave of it earlier at my workplace. This new approach that I had begun, more as an outcome of the plot adventures, pushed me to manage things in a different way without there being a choice, and it had taught me well.

As I was introspecting, one of the new joiners, Matthew, came to me and said in a hushed tone, "Psst Raj." He looked around as if trying to be careful not to be caught engaging in some ghastly act.

I followed suit, "What's up, Matthew?"

"You know the HR people have made me the floor warden."

I didn't know why he was telling me this. But to keep up his spirits, I said, "Many congratulations, buddy."

"Eh...what are you saying? Being the floor warden is one of the worst punishments one can get. I think this is a new way to rag the new joiners in an official way," he said.

"Oh yes, in fact my exact opinion about being a floor warden. But then why did you tell me that?"

"Because one of the activities that floor wardens are involved in is to organise and ensure participation in fire drills."

"That is good. So?" I was puzzled.

He gave me a bad stare. I tell you the work culture has changed so drastically in the past decade. In my fresher days, I used to shut up and blindly listen to my seniors. Today, these young millennials care nothing about hierarchy. If you have to win over them, it has to be by doing something they value and appreciate. Anyway, he continued with his bad stare at me, till I actually registered what he meant.

"You mean, there's a fire drill today?"

"Yes sir! You got that one," he teased.

"But why are you telling me? Aren't you supposed to ensure all of us participate?"

"Dude, listen completely." Yeah, you heard that one right. It is the junior most guy in the team, calling his acting Team Lead 'dude'.

"Sorry for the interruption, sir. Tell me," I said sarcastically.

"It is Preeti's birthday today."

"Oh, really."

"Yeah, but she's not that happy as her fiancé is out of station."

"Oh correct, she got engaged just a few weeks ago."

"Yeah, correct. So she's not all that happy today. I thought you all can take her out during the fire drill, as the Operations Control team does not take into account the fire drill time as productivity loss," he concluded.

"And you?"

"Boss, I am the floor warden. I cannot go missing."

"Wow, that's a nice thought you have there, Matthew."

"Yeah well, see Preeti is a very nice person. She helps all of us so much, and it just doesn't make sense to see her stuck in a fire drill on her birthday, and holding placards asking people to do some random things like – Don't panic during fire, don't take the elevators, use stairs with one hand free, and stuff like that."

"Makes sense, so when is the drill?"

"It is at three. I suggest you leave for late lunch and escape directly from there, and come back by four."

"That sounds like a plan. Appreciate it, warden."

"Not at all. And do you know something funny?"

"No, tell me."

"I got to know this during the floor warden sessions. It seems there is an online request that you need to raise when there is fire."

"Come on Mathew, are you joking?"

"No dude, real serious. I checked that out last week as well. It is one of the drop downs for the online requests. It says 'Fire Alert'." He laughed animatedly.

"So you are saying that if there's fire, instead of running helter-skelter or wait, sorry...instead of following the floor warden to reach a safe spot at the earliest, we are supposed to login to the company website and choose the option 'Fire Alert'," I really couldn't conclude it before laughing animatedly myself.

He had gone crazy doing his mono-acting.

"Fire Fire!" he would say and get up to run for his life, then go up to the door to leave the building, but his face takes a serious expression and he says, "Not before I do this", and comes running to his desktop and says, "Not before I raise the 'Fire Alert' request," and we both could not control laughing out loud. He fell from his chair and continued to laugh though he was on the floor.

When I saw that this was disturbing others, I signalled him to stop it. He then called me to his workstation, and logged into the web link. He then showed me the 'Fire Alert' option as well. Something caught my eye, and I asked him to scroll down to see the various options in the drop-down and found something referred to as 'Mosquitoes'.

This time, it was my turn to fall on the floor and laugh. There was an online request we had to raise if we find mosquitoes at our workstations! After recovering from my fit of laughter, and drying my eyes which had tears, I got an idea. "Matthew, raise the request for mosquitoes. I want to see what they do."

He raised the request, but there was a pop-up window in the end. It said, 'A trigger has been sent for your Supervisor's approval'.

He was unable to believe this. "Are they freaking mad! A mosquito issue requires supervisor's approval?"

Then I saw the name it had been triggered to. Thankfully, it was my name. I went to my laptop and as soon as I saw this request, I approved it and then we decided to wait and watch.

After ten minutes, there was an outsourced contract employee who walked in. He wore his company T-shirt on which the logo read 'Pest-o-kill'. He came to Matthew and asked, "Sir, you raised a request?"

"Yes, I did," said Matthew.

"Where is the mosquito?" he asked.

"It was here, irritating me ten minutes ago."

"No problem. You work, and I will find it," he said, and then I saw him unleash his weapon. He got out an electric bat that resembled a tennis racquet, which I swear I have seen on the main Majestic bus stand footpath being sold for a hundred and fifty bucks. My firm was paying a vendor for a contractor whose job was to come with an electric bat to kill mosquitoes!

He walked slowly, for I guess he didn't want to scare off the mosquito. This is how Arnold Schwarzenegger walks in the movie *Predator*.

Preeti, who hadn't noticed this drama, wasn't aware he was right behind her. She called out to Mathew loudly to come and help her with something. "Shhh...." he said, as she looked back at him surprised. "Please don't move," he said.

She was anyway stunned by his very existence on the Accounts Payable floor that she dared to even breathe. Only after seeing the electric bat in his hand did she realise he was no terrorist who had come into the campus, but was just trying to kill some pests.

He scanned the area for a couple of minutes, and then said to Matthew, "I think it has escaped, sir," and walked to the door.

"No, it's here," shouted Preeti, making all of us turn towards her in surprise.

I gave a sharp look to Matthew. I would have expected him to update me in case he had planted a mosquito. It is a different thing that I had no clue how one can plant a mosquito.

The pest-o-kill guy came back with a vengeance and immediately stopped at his tracks looking at where Preeti was pointing her finger. He looked back at Matthew, "I cannot kill it sir."

I mean really dude! People who come to the war-field and just at the nick of time, when the act needs to happen they refuse to go ahead. Such ghastly acts are intolerable I tell you. Wasn't this exactly what Arjuna went through in Kurukshetra? Just when he saw that he had to wage war against his own blood, he refused to lift his weapon. Moreover, we didn't even have Lord Krishna in the vicinity to help us reveal the duties of an individual, as people without identity card were not allowed in our floor because of client security reasons. We only had Krishnappa, an SME from the neighbouring team. But I personally knew that he had problems giving even simple team debriefing, and hence asking him to make a life-changing speech was expecting too much from that poor chap.

I asked myself, "Why would the pest-o-kill guy not go ahead and do his duty for which the company seemed to be shelling out enough money? He wasn't related to any mosquito!"

But I wouldn't hide this secret from my patient readers. I came back to earth when I heard Matthew speak.

"What happened boss? Why won't you kill the mosquito?" Demanded this young millennial. They ask questions I tell you, a lot. Thankfully, the question was posed to the pest-o-killer and not me. I too added my two bits in between, "Yes, why is that boss? I have approved the request as well."

The pest-o-killer looked at the spot that Preeti had pointed at, and then at Matthew, "Because, sir, it is not a mosquito." He moved away revealing what the issue was.

From the distance that we were seated, I had no clue what he was showing us. It was only Preeti who said, "Oh, okay."

I too added, "Oh, like that", not knowing what it was.

It was Matthew who interrupted, "Like what? I didn't understand folks." He looked at me.

Not having an answer, I didn't know what to say. But I gave a very knowing nod and said, "Tell him Preeti," eager to listen to what it was.

"It is a fly, not a mosquito," she said with a grim face.

"And hence sir…" the pest-o-killer said, "I cannot kill it." He sounded like he was one of those lawyers who in the end proved that his client wasn't guilty and tell the judge, "And the defence rests, your honour."

"So what if it is a fly?" challenged Matthew.

"You raised a request for a mosquito, sir."

"Dude, you really expect us to take a microscope and find out what that small insect was before we raise a request?"

"But sir, I have my boundaries. I am authorised only to follow the exact processes and procedures. I cannot deviate from it," said the pest-o-killer.

"Are you joking man? Next you would say that even with the category of mosquitoes, we need to highlight if the species is Aedes

Albopictus or Anopheles or Asian tiger?" asked Matthew. There was a stunned silence in the bay.

I must admit that I never registered or even thought about the different species of mosquitoes. I do know that it is the female anopheles mosquitoes that transmits malaria from my primary school days. My Ph.D. on mosquitoes begins and ends there.

There was no way the pest-o-killer would have countered this knowledgeable question that Matthew posed, but he behaved his passive aggressive self. "No sir, I will not be able to attack the fly. It is beyond my duties," he said.

Strange as it may seem, but the fly didn't fly away the whole while. Never in its short life of a few weeks had it received so much attention from men, who had nothing else to do in life and were debating on annihilating the insect. So it hung around thinking that we would anyway keep arguing till it was time for it to move on to become something else in its next life.

Mathew threatened that he would complain to the pest-o-killer's supervisor, but the guy didn't budge.

Before Mathew could login into some other complicated web-link to find out the contact details of the supervisor of this guy, I intervened. "Enough!" I said, raising my hand for effect. It worked, I must say, for the neighbouring team again paused from what they were doing and looked at me expectantly.

"Quiet!" I said again.

"But I am standing silently, sir," said the pest-o-killer, lacking the finesse of knowing when to shut up.

I ignored him, and turned to Matthew, "Show the request that you raised. Now!" Of course I added the exclamation only to scare the pest-o-kill guy, and hoped Matthew understood it.

The way he acted all helpless and said, "Yes, sir. I am checking." I knew he understood I was on to something.

"Here, sir", he said when he opened the online request. I went to him, but my eyes were on the pest-o-kill guy. Because of that I banged my left foot on to the chair that Matthew was sitting on, and Preeti made a face registering it must have hurt. It did hurt, but there was no way I would show that on my face. I decided that I would look into it once this matter was closed, and asked Mathew to go to the drop-down options, which he did.

"Come here," I called the pest-o-kill guy, and he readily came.

"Show me the option that we need to choose for housefly in this drop-down," I told him, and went around for a stroll. I returned to Matthew's seat and saw the pest-o-killer looking baffled, for during his denial to do his duty, I vaguely remembered that I had gone through all other options in the drop-down before asking Matthew to raise a request for mosquito, and there surely was no mention of any housefly there.

Matthew by now knew where this was going, and winked at me knowingly. I was learning the tricks of impressing young millennials this way.

"I am sorry, sir. There is no option for firefly."

"Housefly."

"Yes, no option for housefly, sir."

"Then instead of just going ahead and doing your job, you are sitting here and wasting all our time? Do you know the total productivity loss you are responsible for can run into lakhs of rupees? Will you go ahead and do your duty without further argument or do you want to take the responsibility of the loss your lack of action is causing?"

He didn't wait for me to finish, and sprung with the electric tennis bat, like Rafael Nadal would do before his serve. The housefly, quick to join in the game, flew from its place near Preeti and went up to Matthew's place. Recovering from his near fall, the pest-o-killer passed the electric bat to the left hand and tried a backhand swing which missed the housefly, Matthew and his chair, by a big margin, the way Glen McGrath used to miss the ball when he had to come out to bat as the number eleven.

My reflexes are neither as good as Matthew's as he ducked the pest-o-killer's swing nor as good as the fly's that missed his onslaught. So I was worried thinking it might reach my seat and I will have invited trouble in the form of pest-o-killer by having rubbed him the wrong way. Even if he missed hitting the fly, because of the frustration that I had managed to build in him by shouting at him, I knew there was a strong possibility that he might take a big swing at me if the fly even managed to come anywhere in the vicinity of two metres from me.

Thankfully, the fly chose to forgive all the push I had done to put the pest-o-killer on the job, and moved on to the neighbouring team. The pest-o-killer's ego was hurt now, as he had missed getting the fly a couple of times already. Like a bull enraged, he charged from Matthew's seat and jumping over the divider, he fell on the carpet on the other side with a thud.

All of us gasped and got up to see if he had done any damage to himself. He, too proud to show if he'd been affected by any injury the way I had done earlier, got up on his feet and searched for the fly.

The bay in which we were seated was a reasonably big one, accommodating some forty-five of us. The fly flew to the other end where the main entrance to the bay was. The pest-o-killer, knowing this was the last chance he had, ran behind it. Little did he know that the door would be pushed open by someone, which made the fly reverse its direction and settle between his legs. The only swing option left for him was the tweener, and he swung the bat between his legs. He was no Boris Becker to pull up a fast one this way, and in the momentum, the bat got entangled between his legs and he rolled out of the bay, giving a grand ending to the adventure.

It was time for lunch soon, and some of us from the team asked Preeti to join us for lunch outside, to which she was extremely happy. Matthew unfortunately had to stay back for the fire drill.

As there were many of us, Preeti suggested we go in her car, which surprised me, for I hadn't known she owned a car.

While we were on the way to a restaurant, we spoke freely, and judging by the conversations, it dawned upon me that she was from quite a well-off family. It was also clear that unlike most of us, she didn't necessarily have to work for a living, but did so because she wanted to.

Nice kid, I thought. Also then I thought about the upcoming promotion recommendations. She was an excellent performer and also was eligible for the next level. Only that it meant she would have to move out of the team as I was already the SME in our team, which would put the team in jeopardy. Nevertheless, I made a mental note that I should bring this up with my supervisor when I spoke to him next, much before the promotion cycle.

"Do you mind if I put on the radio?" I asked Preeti.

"Not at all. Please go ahead."

I switched it on, without knowing the volume was tuned too low. It was Shreyal Ghosal's voice, which I like very much. I then increased the volume, and gasped a bit as there was a voice over of her breathing very heavily and then *"Ooh la la, ooh la la"*, began Bappi Lahiri. I immediately changed the channel before there was any embarrassment in the car.

Then before I could register, *"Mein Zandu balm hui, darling tere liye"* played up. I again changed it without waiting for long. Never when I am at home and scanning all music channels would I see item songs pop up this way. But it was all happening now.

There were advertisements on one of those channels, which I felt was best under the present circumstances. I almost jumped up in my seat, as the lady began to explain how soft and tender the legs were, and felt extremely scandalised as I was amidst girls in the car. One of the brave-hearts from behind said, "Chill Raj, she is talking about chicken kebabs."

"Yes, of course. I think I will switch it off though." There was stunned silence for a bit in the car, but thankfully the girls behind began to talk amongst themselves, and I could breathe easy.

"So you've been traveling out of Bangalore lately, and in fact taking breaks in between, Raj. I hope you are not applying to other jobs," asked Preeti as the girls in the backseat were busy discussing some pattern or colour of something that I wished not to be a part of.

"Ha ha! How I wish Preeti!"

"What? Why? What have we done to you that you have to look out for a job?"

"No, I was just kidding." I thought for a moment and then decided that it was okay to tell her about my endeavour to buy a plot.

"Oh, that's nice. Have you finalised any?" she questioned.

"Not actually. Each plot I visited had some or the other issue."

"If you don't mind, can I suggest something?"

"Yes, sure go ahead."

"One of my cousins returned after working for almost four years in the US. He had some good savings and wanted to put it in the right place. He did a lot of research, and his family has good contacts as well, you see. He zeroed in on a big piece of land recently. His family also has a good lawyer as a family friend. He looked into all aspects and found everything to be quite alright. If you want to consider this, I can get the contact details."

"But Preeti, you say it's a big plot, and also don't think I am judging, but if your cousin has worked in the US for years and has done some savings, it surely won't be comparable to what I can afford."

"I get it Raj, but see, my cousin is not taking any loan at all. He is going ahead with full payment out of his savings. So I am sure, with bank loan, you should be able to get this one. He had taken me there a couple of weeks ago before he finalised it. After all, what's the harm in visiting it once?"

"Hmm....sure Preeti. It will help if you can get me the contact details."

It was surely a class 'A' place what Preeti's cousin had bought. In fact, it again was on the Sarjapur Road, but not anywhere close to what I had gone through recently. There were no Tirumala bars to be located and no Kaka tea stall to be visited.

It was a bit further off from the city, yes. But the promoter was upfront about it from the very beginning, and also took all my questions without any qualms.

"See Mr Raj, people advertise in papers or on radio or on hoardings stating 'last few plots available' and things like that. But think about it, if there are only last few plots that are left and they are selling like hot cakes, why do they need paid advertisements in the first place?"

I saw a point in what he said.

"I am not going to have any sale pitch on this one. We have done good work on these plots and it is here for you to see with your own eyes. We have been lucky that many of our customers have spread the news to people whom they know and we are surely not worried about not being able to sell these plots."

It was an extremely easy conversation to have with the promoter, Mr Jain. He was in no hurry and as he already mentioned, I didn't find him to be very jumpy either.

He further explained, "Also Mr Raj, there is a key reason why the plots are not very highly priced and I don't want there to be any gap in understanding about that. So these are huge plots if you can see. However, the scheme is such that there will be three fourths of the plot dedicated for vegetation or agriculture purpose, and the remainder one fourth is where you will be able to construct the villa. As per our contract, we will have no issues taking care of the garden or orchard. The output will be split 70:30 in your favour, and we will keep the remainder thirty percent as our service charges. This will continue up to five years from the date of registration. Post that, the promoters will withdraw, letting the customers form a society and that society will take over all such maintenance activities. Please let me know if you need any clarification."

"Mr Jain, though you have not priced the project very highly, considering it is a big plot, the total cost for me will work out quite high. So I wanted to understand if there are loan opportunities available at all."

"Of course there is. But if I may suggest this? What's in front of us, is the bigger version of the plot. We also have a slightly small set of plots available that I would like to show to you in the same property. Nothing changes in terms of services or contract between the two. See if you want to look at that as well and then make your final decision. I understand you have my number. I will be happy to help," he offered.

"Thanks for being direct on some of these points, Mr Jain. It really helps people like me take a decision. One more question I had for you, sir."

"Yes, please go ahead."

"So which banks do you have a tie-up with?"

"Oh yes, sorry I missed mentioning that. One of them is FDPL bank, and the other is a co-operative bank."

"Hmm...How come co-operative banks are giving these loans? That is not heard of."

"Yes, you are right in saying that. See, there's nothing called Land loan, all the housing related loans are disbursed by selected private banks. However, considering this is a new concept coming up in housing, where we are kind of blending in the cultivation aspect, our legal team recommended that it makes sense to partner with one of the co-operative banks as well."

"That's interesting. And the loans are provided for only by these two banks I presume?"

"Saying that would not be right. But the point is this, as we have done our tie-up with these two, it is much easier for us to process the documentation from both the bank perspective and the developer's perspective. The master documentation on the land and other prominent papers would have already been handed over to these two banks. Hence, I would recommend you try and work with one of them."

"Understand, makes sense. Thanks again."

My father went through all the details, and was quite impressed with the quality that these developers had maintained. "Looks okay to me, Raj. But the big plots are out of question. We will not be able to afford it."

"That's true Dad, but I was very keen on the smaller ones. The dimensions aren't too small either."

"Hmm...true. It is an interesting thing though. So only one-fourth of the land is where you can construct the house and remaining has to be left for cultivation purpose."

"That's okay Dad. I still feel it is a good deal. And I am sure that in the long term, if need be, there will be some provision for us to convert a part of the three-fourth land for construction."

"Yes, I agree. We can explore that in the future. It is not that you are going to construct the house immediately."

"Yeah, look at me. Firstly let me get a hand on a piece of land, and finish off with that loan."

"Instead, I am thinking aloud, why don't you leave this land business and get an apartment?"

"Stop talking like Sandhya, Dad!" I blurted out, as I clenched my fist, hoping he didn't get the drift.

"That reminds me, how is Sandhya? I have not seen her for some months now. Hope she is doing well."

"Ahem...she's kind of out of touch Dad. Must be doing fine."

"And how is Mr Johnathon, her father?"

"It is Mr Johansson Dad. I guess he must be fine as well."

"It was almost a year ago that we all had met in that marriage of a friend of yours. It was a nice get-together."

"Okay so Dad, I will understand my loan eligibility from the banks. They have two banks that they have tied up with."

"Sorry? Oh yes! We should do that. Good to see you are doing things alone. It's as if you have become a different person in a few months," my father observed.

"Did Mrs Anu say anything about the amount they need to pay us?"

"How forgetful of me! Yes, she did."

"That's okay. What did she say? They need one more month, is it?"

"So, she said that we need not travel this weekend to Mysore."

"What a subtle way of saying they need more time."

"No, listen. She said that she will send out a courier with the cheque for nearly half the amount in a couple of days. The remainder of the amount will be paid in cash it seems, for some internal tax purpose. I am sure they are doing some avoidance of tax. But that is not our problem for now. I have told her to cross the cheque before she sends..."

"Wow, wait Dad, that is some good news, isn't it?"

"Huh? Yes, it is. But it is not over until it is over, Raj. I agree it is a good sign, but don't be too happy till all the money is deposited into your account. Didn't you see how that Nair could change his colour like a chameleon the last time we met him. Never trust anyone in matters of money."

"Hmm...makes sense. Let us wait for them to send out the cheque then."

▲

It was a Saturday, and as we had no reasons to travel to Mysore to meet the Nairs, I decided to first visit FDPL bank. Somehow I have always had an allergy to public or co-operative sectors. So I saved the co-operative bank only as back-up.

Though I felt it was on the outskirts of the city, the FDPL bank had a very impressive office. As soon as I entered, the first observation was that there were more bank employees than the customers. That thankfully worked to my advantage, as there was someone to attend to me in a minute.

"Good morning Mr Raj. I am Anand, the relationship manager for the project that Mr Jain is working on. It seems you wanted to see me."

"Hi Mr Anand, yes. Mr Jain recommended your name regarding loan for those plots."

"I will just give you a checklist of items that you need to have and details you need to fill. Once that is done, we can catch up. It shouldn't take you more than ten minutes to fill this."

"I will do that, thanks."

It was quite a big checklist with small font, and I had trouble reading. I thought I'd get my eyes checked when I got time. As I went through the details I needed to furnish, it made me feel a bit offended. Of course, there was no fault in them asking me about my monthly salary slips, my bonus amount, offer letter, revision letter and so on. Just that I as a person am not very outspoken about these details, and hence felt a bit uncomfortable. But I knew it was an obvious set of details I had to fill in. Once I was done filling and went to Mr Anand, it gave me an uneasy sensation of letting my deepest secrets know to some stranger. But once Mr Anand took it, he hardly glanced at it and called out his assistant to do some calculations and got busy with other stuff.

"Sir, my assistant will calculate and tell you the loan eligibility. Meanwhile, let me fill you in with the documents that I will need from you."

"Sure, let me make a note of it. Just a minute." I got out my notepad and pen. No, I am not someone so diligent to carry all these anywhere. In fact, I hardly take a notepad even to the team meetings in office, and I have gotten proper scolding from my supervisor in the past. Thanks to my Dad, who told me to ensure I take these things and diligently make a note of each point, as I will not know which one will end up being an important one.

It actually made a lot of sense the way he put it, and especially considering this was a matter of loan worth lakhs of rupees, there was every reason for me to be extra cautious.

"So, I will need your attested copies for last six months' bank statements. I mean, the one where you have your salary account."

"Is it? Six months' statements?"

Surprised at being interrupted, he looked up to me matter-of-factly and nodded his head. I gave a consent by nodding in return, but giving my bank account statements did make me feel a bit touchy.

He went on, "Are you married, sir?"

"No, why?"

"We will need a co-applicant."

"Okay, will my father do?"

"Yes, that should be fine. You will need to submit last two financial years' Form 16, attested by the approved authority in your company's finance team, proof of all investments you have in your name, proof of any loan – vehicle, house, personal – that you may be under, and the set of documents you already saw in the form you filled that are related to your present job – that is, your salary slips, offer letter, revision letter – all attested by someone from the HR department of your company."

It had been several years since I had made such quick notes. I had mentally switched off getting surprised with the kind of details that were being asked. I think I would as well have agreed to give if he had next asked me what the size of my vests and briefs were. I sat back and thought about the reactions my body was going through. I was breathing very heavily, and there was a slight shiver in my left leg.

"And yes, I am sorry, I forgot to mention one more thing, sir. I will also need six cheque leafs from your bank where you have the salary account."

"Six cheque leafs?" I was surprised.

"Yes sir, six leafs – One with the single EMI, I mean the Equal Monthly Instalment amount mentioned, three with the EMI details multiplied by three, and the last two will be blank cheques – all of which drawn in the name of FDPL bank housing finance limited."

"Sorry, I mean, it may sound dumb, but why are these needed?"

"Sir, it is a natural question. There may be few instances where people default the payments. We use these cheques in such situations."

"No, I understood that. But why blank cheques?"

"Sir, for the same purpose again. This will be used in case of repeated defaulting."

"Then I can write the maximum amount on it, no?"

He just casually smiled. "Sir I understand your concern, but that is the standard format. In fact, I recommend you to call up other banks and check with them on the process. It will be hardly any different."

"Phew..." this was getting too stuffy. The only thing pending after all these details was for me to sign up my soul and give it to the bank for mortgage. I am sure the writer of movie *Ghost Rider* had a similar experience with the housing loan and got the idea of making the character sign up his soul.

As I was letting this information sink in, and Mr Anand cleverly behaved as if he was looking into some other papers, clearly giving me time to recover, the assistant whom he had asked to do some calculations returned with some notes of his own.

"Ah, yes. Here, sir. Considering your current salary details, age, and the vehicle loan that you are paying back, this is the approximate loan amount you will be eligible for. I repeat that this is approximate, and that on furnishing the detailed proofs that we just discussed, I will be able to comment on the exact value."

I nodded and took the calculation details mentioned on a note pad. I spoke as soon as I saw that, "But this is not the maximum loan amount, is it?"

"Ah, yes sir. That is basis your loan eligibility."

I continued to look at the piece of paper. Not that I had not registered the details given initially, but to avoid my expressions that would have given away how I was feeling. The loan amount that I was eligible for was not even half of what I needed to make this deal happen. This point never struck me earlier that I could not be eligible for the maximum loan I needed.

"Uff...Is there any possibility of this increasing to whatever extent Mr Anand?"

He calmly shook his head, "I am really sorry, sir. Those parameters are fixed at the bank level. I don't think we will be able to increase that any further."

I smiled a difficult smile. "In that case Mr Anand, it will be difficult for me to go ahead with the loan."

By his expression, he understood. "I will once anyway talk to my higher-ups, sir. But I will be honest here, that I have never seen these parameters being negotiated. But I will try once."

"No that's okay Mr Anand. Don't waste your time on it. I will try for a different property, and in case your bank is tied up with them, I will come back to you again."

"Sure sir, anytime. Thank you."

I felt very little walking out of the bank. Gone was that false sense of pride in me. I had been subtly shown my place. I didn't know if it made sense to go to Janaka Seva Co-operative Bank to speak about the loan. That was when Anand came running to me, "Sir, I hope you will visit Janaka Seva Co-operative bank. They have higher coverage is what many customers have told me. I don't mean a small difference. I mean cases like you where people are looking for a much higher coverage."

"Oh, that is some decent news Mr Anand. Appreciate this gesture."

I smiled at the genuine concern this guy was showing as he returned to his desk.

"So Janaka Seva Co-operative Bank it is," I told myself and went asking the route.

No sooner than I entered, I felt it was an old government office. I remember being in one such place in my childhood, which was more of a labyrinth with walls of steel. It had been very claustrophobic and an overwhelming experience.

There were many customers in the bank, though I had no clue what they were trying to do. I was sure that not everyone present there had come to acquire a loan for the same set of plots. Or was it the case? Shoot! Then I better hurry up before all the plots are taken up. What was happening to me? I sat on the metal chair as soon as an elderly gentleman left it and tried to calm myself.

Was this anxiety? Was I so tired and fatigued? Oh man, was I growing old sooner than I thought? Deep breath Raj, deep breath.

After timing and spending at least five minutes at the chair to organise my thoughts is when I got up to find out the needed details. Trust such sectors to be unorganised, and they will stand up to the occasion. There were some eight tables, and only three of them occupied with customers rushing at each of the tables. This I felt would take a lot of time. But then I saw the fourth bank employee return from his lunch. I thought I should catch him before he decided to leave for tea.

"Sir, one minute."

"Hmm...?" He wouldn't look at me.

"I have come to ask details about loan for Mr Jain's plots, sir."

This got his attention, and he viewed me keenly. There was no pretence about it. He was trying to make out something about me as he scanned me from head to toe, and spoke, "But I was told they have tied up with FDPL bank, and most of the people are going there."

"Is it? I don't know about that sir. As soon as I heard that a co-operative bank is giving a loan, I rushed here."

"Ha!" He let out a lazy laugh, and continued to clean his ears. I didn't want to mention it earlier, but he just wouldn't let his ear go. He was holding on to it with all his might. Even my school teachers, on me not completing my homework, the occurrence of which was quite common, never held my ear for such a long time.

"Yes sir?" I asked as he was not willing to speak after his 'Ha'.

"All these private banks are the same. They will loot you with high rate of interest and have malpractices to lure customers. Only when the customer is completely trapped in their hold that they reveal their true colours," he said.

I didn't know what to say and nodded along. "Sir, whom can I speak about it?"

"I don't know." He began to walk away.

"Sir sir, please let me know."

"No I am not joking kid. I really don't know. Our branch manager has not nominated anyone for this yet. I only heard that a couple of cases from Mr Jain that came to our bank were handled directly by our branch manager. See if you want to speak to him." He indicated towards a glass door and continued walking with his pot belly waving from one table to another.

I wasted no time and went to the cabin. The name plate read 'Baskhar, Branch Manager'. Though it was a glass door, it had translucent plastic coating and hence it was difficult to know if it was occupied. I waited for half a minute after knocking, and then knocked again. This time a bit louder and called out, "May I come in, sir?"

"Who is it?" came the voice.

"A customer, sir."

"Come in."

I entered the cabin, to see that it was occupied by two individuals. I said, "Sir...I was asked to meet with the branch manager, Mr Baskhar."

"What's this regarding?" one of them spoke and I guessed it was him.

"Mr Jain sent me here sir. This was related to loan for the plot of land."

"But why didn't you go to FDPL?"

"Sir, I thought co-operative banks are better."

"Hmm...Sit down."

"Thanks, sir."

"How much loan do you want?"

"The maximum extent, sir."

"How much do you make monthly?" The language he used was surely not polished. Nevertheless, I told him my salary details.

"Only so much. Why will we give you loan up to the maximum amount then?"

I didn't know what to answer. Before I could saying anything, he went on, "Which company do you work for? What's your age?" he asked, extremely irritated with my presence, or maybe my whole existence.

I promptly told him, totally ignoring his lack of interest. Maybe he just wanted to check how badly I needed the loan.

He expression changed immediately, "Show me your salary slips," he commanded.

I removed the latest salary slip from the file I was carrying and handed it over to him.

"I knew it! You are in BPO!"

"Yes, Mr Baskhar. That is correct, sir," I couldn't understand the reason for his jubilation.

"How did you think we will give you a loan?"

"Excuse me sir?"

"We don't give loan to BPO people, boss."

"Why sir? I don't follow."

"How do you think you will be able to repay such big loans with a BPO job? We would have considered if you were a software engineer. But BPO and all, please don't come to us. We cannot process any loan for you people."

He put the salary slips on the table, and immediately addressed the other individual sitting next to him, "My cousin sister's daughter got an alliance in marriage from a BPO employee last year, and they agreed for it without consulting me once. Today, the husband works in night shifts. Tell me, why she had to take such a stupid step?"

The other one didn't understand a thing, but chimed in the expected expressions.

"I don't understand the reason. You think I don't get monthly salary to repay you or something like that?"

"Watch your tone, young man."

"Why, if I watch it, will you give me the loan?"

"Huh? If you don't lower you voice, I will call security."

I was now done putting up with this guy. I thought I should once take a deep breath, and I did. I was right. Nothing else would make sense. "Look moron, firstly I had not come asking for a favour or begging you for alms. It is a bloody loan, which I would have paid back with interest. If you cannot freaking lend me the loan, then say it in bloody simple words and I will leave. You don't have to behave like a jerk," I said each word with cold clarity so that he could not miss any of it.

"I will call security! How dare you use such words at me?"

"Trust me when I say that I would have used even stronger, juicier and meatier words. Only that my stupid author wouldn't let me. Got it? Bloody Baskhard."

Call me a fool to have done this, but I would not have been able to look at myself in the eye had it ended in any other way.

"Hmm...you said all these to him, is it? Or you are making it up now?" asked my father, perhaps unable to comprehend why I spoke to the branch manager that way.

"Dad...I really don't think I was unreasonable."

My father nodded. "I agree with you."

"Oh, you do?" Of course I was surprised.

"I mean...people in these sectors at times go on power trips, and think they are above everyone. At times they need instances to bring them back on earth. And out-rightly insulting people the way he did with you, is surely not right."

"Thanks Dad."

"I am only glad you didn't end up slapping him or something. It would then have become a police case," and he laughed, much to my relief.

"What next Dad?"

"I actually don't know son. Let's leave this here for now, and think about it tomorrow."

"I am sorry, Dad."

My father rested his hand on my shoulder, "There's nothing to be sorry about."

I couldn't sleep that night. I tossed around in my bed till midnight when I received a ping on my phone.

"Which idiot is sending messages at this hour?" I cursed under my breath and saw that it was a message from Prakhar. It would be morning for him.

You awake? the message read.

I decided to call him up, "What's up bugger?"

"Hey dude, it must be around twelve in the night for you."

"It is."

"How come you are still awake? All okay?"

"Well, yeah. Why do you ask?"

"Nothing, I just had a bad feeling, and thought I should just check."

"Wow, now you are getting into telepathy and stuff Prakhar. Nothing that's out of whack, but yes, I have not been feeling great."

"Why? Is it about the plot thing you were working on?" The good part about best friends is that they just seem to get the pulse, and no matter even if you are talking after a long break, you pick things up where you'd left.

"Yeah dude, it's kind of frustrating."

"Why do you say that? I thought you said there are a few short-listed by Uncle, and you would be visiting some of them. You didn't like any?"

"Not exactly man. I think I am done with it."

"What are you talking Raj? Speak clearly."

"This land thing ya. I...I don't think it's in my fate."

"You are scaring me now. Since when did you start talking about fate and stuff?"

"It's a joke how things panned out Prakhar, and the joke is on me. Nothing's fallen in place dude. Just nothing. The last few months have made me shed all my false pride and I think I have fallen to the ground, face first. And guess what? The ground does not belong to me. That plot's been taken by someone else," I added sarcastically.

"It's just property Raj. There will be many more such opportunities. Why do you speak as if this is the end?"

"I don't think so. I surely don't have it in me to do this anymore. And trust me, I am not accepting defeat with just one experience. I tried multiple projects, but not even a single thing worked in my favour man, and when I almost thought I had found something good, these bank morons refused to process my loan. They say they don't give loans to BPO employees. I mean that's insane."

"Really? Which idiot makes those rules?"

"I swear man."

"Listen, if it is the matter of the loan where you are stuck, then let me lend you some money," he offered without thinking twice.

My answer too didn't take long. "Nope."

"What? I will lend you money, I said."

"No Prakhar. I will not take money from you."

"Dude, I am not doing any personal favour right? I am lending it to you. You return when you are able to."

"I will not take money from you, Prakhar."

"But why?"

"Dude, I have seen this happen with many, including my father. You involve money in friendship, you lose the money as well as the friendship. I cannot lose you man."

"What rubbish bromance you are doing. I will transfer the money to you and..."

"Prakhar, that conversation has ended. I cannot involve money between us."

"But..."

"No! Please. Let's talk about something else."

"Hmm...Any idea how's Sandhya?"

"No dude, have not spoken to her in several months. I guess she's moved on quite well."

"But you haven't moved on."

"Huh...of course I have moved on as well."

"Don't talk like a moron. It is obvious you have not moved on."

"I mean...It's ended for good, man."

"How do you mean? For whose good?"

"For her own good Prakhar. She's...she's way good for me. She deserves someone much better. I hope she's found him."

"Don't under-rate yourself so much, Raj."

"In fact, it's the other way round. I think I had over-rated myself for a long time. The last some months have given me the beating of my life. And guess what? Even here, she was right, isn't it? Sandhya was the one who kept telling me to invest in some property, and we argued over that every time. In fact, that was the reason why we broke up as well. When I started with the property search, I thought it was just an exaggeration that people do. With each property I experienced a different kind of failure, Prakhar. It shattered my ego into little pieces man. Along with my ego, it shattered me as well I guess."

Prakhar didn't speak a word, as I continued, "Look at my bloody audacity, that I insulted my father for the plot he bought decades ago saying it was a bad decision. I am not even eligible to get a plot outside the city. This is all I am worth!"

"You are being too harsh. You are way more worthy than what you are assessing yourself right now. You are feeling very low, which is influencing your state of mind."

"I don't know man. I think I will leave all this shit behind and focus on work. I think I have learnt my lessons that I had to from these experiences."

"Listen to me Raj. You are not going to die tomorrow or something. You still are young and have a long life ahead of you. I cannot agree with you the way you are aligning the measure of your success with a property. If that's the case, even I don't own a thing."

"But didn't you listen to me Prakhar? You are a techie dude. Tomorrow, you at least have that Baskhar who will more than willingly give you loan to purchase land!" We laughed at the silly joke.

"Raj, I think you should talk to Sandhya once."

"For what, Prakhar? She would have moved on and maybe she's with someone already. I cannot do this to her. As much as I hated her all these months for being right in every instance, I just know I am not the right guy for her."

"You can call her and if your relation wasn't ever meant to be, at least end it in the right way dude. The way you broke up with her was very immature."

"Hey! I thought you are my friend!"

"Yes, I am. That's why I am telling you to do it."

"I don't know Prakhar. I don't think I have the guts."

"At least think about it."

"Hmm...If I don't say that, you will not put the bloody phone down, will you?"

"Yeah, that's correct."

"Oh, good lord. With friends like you, I don't need enemies."

"Okay, cut the crap and come to the point. I am not your supervisor at work that you will faff around unnecessarily."

"Woah! Okay sir. I will try. Okay?"

"Yeah, that's better. Listen I also wanted to tell you that I might come down to Bangalore in a couple of months."

"What! And you saved that for the last?"

"Yeah, I just had to make you feel special for a moment, so that you think I have called you to help you vent out all rubbish that you were imagining. Now that is done, and I see you are feeling better, I am coming to the point."

"My goodness! You will rot in hell man."

"Yeah yeah, I know I will be right next to you in hell as well. So I wanted to inform you about my visit. I don't have exact dates though. I will message you once I get to know about it, okay?"

"Cool, great! Will wait for you then."

That bugger was right! After putting out all the rubbish that had been bothering me and had pent up without my knowledge, I was feeling much lighter. The best thing about friends being there is exactly that – they're there. I didn't even realise when I went into a deep slumber.

The beginning of next week had the good news of Mrs Anu sending us the cheque, and the bigger good news that the cheque hadn't bounced. The next tranche of pay-out, which was supposed to be paid out in cash, would be done in a fortnight is what my father was informed. I just kept my fingers crossed that all the amount should be paid without any further complications.

I surely did miss there being no other plot of land or any other property that I needed to visit that week, which was a joke that my father, I and Prakhar shared. I also knew that these plotty experiences had brought me closer to my father, and I began to appreciate his decisions. It is a different thing that I will not be able to understand how he got conned into buying a plot of land next to a running sewerage, but hey! People are allowed to make mistakes in their lives.

I was very lively at office as well, for reasons unknown to me. Maybe after life shows you the uglier side of things, you begin to appreciate the normalcy and start consciously respecting that.

Preeti, my favourite team member, came to me that day, "What happened to the plot you had gone to visit Raj? Was Mr Jain any helpful?"

"Gem of a guy, Preeti. Thank you for helping me with his contacts. But I won't be able to go through with it further. The bank folks just hate me for some reason."

"Oh, I am sorry to hear that."

"No problem at all. How's your fiancé doing?"

She blushed, "He's come down for a week or so. He's doing fine."

"Good to hear that. What about the marriage dates? Are they finalised?"

"Yes yes, they are. It is roughly after five months."

"I hope you will not fly off leaving the company after marriage."

"No, I won't. He'll settle down in Bangalore. So I'll be very much here."

"Okay, great then!"

"Ahem...I thought I will approach you on a later date on this one, but I just wanted to check if I could get a week's leave for my marriage?"

"Yes, of course Preeti! It's your wedding after all. You will have it only once in your life. I suggest you plan your work well ahead and see if you need to take some more days. Please take at least a couple of weeks."

"Yes, in fact there were some three dates shown to us. I chose the date where there was no month-end or quarter-end."

"Dear god Preeti! Relax, it's all well. Please take more leave as you feel appropriate."

"Sure, thanks Raj."

As soon as she left me, I remembered that I hadn't heard back on the final promotion list, in which I had asked my supervisor to recommend Preeti's name. I immediately went up to him. "Ranga, what happened to Preeti's promotion recommendation?" I whispered, as we were on the floor.

"I think it must go through. In fact, I had to get a response from the HR last Friday. Good you reminded me. Let me check with the HR and get back."

In a couple of days, Ranga came to me, "Listen Raj, Preeti's promotion has gone through. The formal communication has come to me. She is now an SME!"

"That's brilliant news Ranga. Has it been communicated? Can I congratulate her?"

"No, it's not been communicated. I thought it was more appropriate if you communicate it to her."

"Eh...me? I...thought there is a protocol that only the supervisor should do the communication."

"That's true. But the way you had built a very strong business case for her, the management had no second thoughts about her promotion. See I will announce it anyway in our team meeting tomorrow. But I thought it will be a very nice thing if you told this to her. Is that okay?"

"That's actually very sweet of you Ranga." I never had thought I would say this to my supervisor ever. He and I were always on the same side. I just never saw it that way in the past.

"What!" shouted Preeti with a lot of excitement in the pantry. "I hadn't expected it to happen this year!"

She was in a state of shock visibly. She had tears in her eyes, which I hadn't expected to see. It is a wonderful feeling when the news you tell someone brings tears of joy. I was just having my first experience of it right now. "I am sorry. It's just so..."

"Not at all. It is very well deserved Preeti. Keep it up. The announcement will happen tomorrow in the team meeting."

The next day, as it was planned, after the team meeting, Ranga asked the group to be seated and announced Preeti's promotion. When she thanked and spoke for a minute, she specially thanked me for my mentoring which helped her, which kind of embarrassed me, and I smiled coyly sitting in one corner.

"Also guys, before we go..." Ranga wasn't done, "Also wanted to share with you one more thing. Raj has been promoted to a Team Leader"

"*What!*"

Yeah, I said it out loud. Everyone seemed so happy and were clapping to my surprise. Preeti and Matthew gave me a friendly hug, as I still was coming to terms with what was happening. All team members came to congratulate me.

As the wishes kept flying, Ranga came to me and said, "I thought of letting you know yesterday, but then again felt this would have been a better way to surprise you. Very well deserved. You have upped the bar in the last couple of quarters. Your team loves you as well. You are in a very enviable place right now, my friend," he said with a genuine smile. I just thanked everyone with the same mechanical smile, for this was new to me. I had seen promotions in the past, but to me this indeed was a real special milestone. I chose silence in accepting all wishes, for I didn't want to open my mouth and make a fool out of myself by saying something stupid.

Once the team disbursed, I stepped out and called up my father and then Prakhar, waking him up at some godforsaken hour in the US. Both were extremely happy for me.

I sat at home, the euphoria in me slightly subsided, having my phone in front of me, and a question in my mind – whether I should call Sandhya or not?

What if she disconnects my call or doesn't receive it at all? What if she receives the call and hurls curses at me and starts insulting me? My body was shivering with these thoughts. But Prakhar had said one thing that was very true. If it was anyway meant to end, the least I should do is to end it amicably.

I took a deep breath, and dialled her number. It was 9:30 p.m. and I knew she liked to sleep before ten. I was hoping she'd not slept. After a few rings, in the middle of which I was tempted to cut the call, she received the call.

"Hello," the voice sounded different. Had she given the phone to someone else to avoid talking to me?

"Eh...Hi...I...Is this Sandhya? Johansson?"

"Yes."

I thought then that she might have deleted my number from her list and might not know who was calling. "This is Raj Setty." I had no clue why I was dealing with the last names here.

"Yes," she said. I could not read anything from the tone. It was neutral.

"Hope it is not too late at night."

"It is," she said.

"Oh okay, no problem. I...I will call tomorrow then."

"What is it?"

"Nothing...Nothing...I just wanted to call you."

"And do what?"

I was silent for a moment, at a loss of words. It was difficult for me to even gulp. "Nothing Sandhya." I remained silent.

This obviously would irritate anyone. "Why did you call?" Now the anger began to surface. I didn't respond.

"With what intention have you called Raj?" she was not hiding her anger anymore and was getting restless as well.

"Listen Sandhya...I am...I am sorry"

"Pathetic! You call me eight months after breaking up with me to say 'sorry'? You think it is so simple?"

"No Sandhya, it is not like that."

"What else is it like Mr Setty? You want to satisfy your ego by saying sorry now?"

"What are you saying Sandhya?"

"Forget what I am saying. Why the hell have you called? What are you trying to say?"

"I am just..."

"What?"

"I just called up...to tell you that I have realised you were right; always."

She was breathing heavily on the other side.

I continued, "And that I was so wrong. I was wrong to not see that you meant well for me. I wanted to tell you that you were always the more mature one between us. Sandhya, I...I went through my own journey in the past few months, and I hated every time...every time remembering that I was a fool to have misunderstood you. You know how you were talking about investing in an apartment and were telling me that I was not taking things seriously. Back then I was blinded by my own over-confidence. I was blinded to think that it was not a big deal to get a property in my name.

"However silly it may sound, but I took up the same eight months ago as a point to prove. To prove it to you that you were wrong, and also to prove to myself that I am no less than others. I did prove a point in the end, after all. I proved to myself that I was nothing but a bloody over-confident fool, Sandhya.

"The experiences showed me that I was a nobody. My ego was ripped apart, and kicked all over. And please don't think that I am saying this so that I can gain compassion from you. No. I just wanted you to know that I have realised I was a moron of the highest order to have broken up with you. I just wanted to acknowledge the fact that now I have clearly understood that it was I who got things completely wrong.

"I don't have anything else to say. Only that you are one of the most wonderful people I have ever met. You deserve all the happiness in the world. I'm glad you've moved on. I wish you find a deserving partner. And lastly, I just wanted you to know that you were the best thing that ever happened to me, and I will cherish that all my life. Bye...Sandhya." I disconnected the call after waiting for a few seconds.

My head throbbed with pain, as if it were being plundered by a hammer. I considered calling Prakhar, but didn't. I curled into a foetal position and tried to sleep.

"How cheap of you that you broke up with Sandhya of all people, Raj? I am ashamed I considered you my mentor," said Preeti.

Ranga followed, "So this is what you really are behind that mask? I will immediately talk to HR if your promotion can be reversed."

It was one of those few instances when I knew I was in the middle of a dream, or a nightmare in this case. But I just went with the flow.

Pramod wasn't happy either, "I and my girlfriend considered you as our idol, man. I hope you take one of the plots from the property I recommended, and you get sued in the court of law."

Matthew said, "Dude, really? Grow up man. I can handle my relationships better than you"

My father was not far behind, "I think I will ask Revathi's hand for you in marriage, Raj." His phone then rang, and he showed it to me and said, "See Revathi's father is calling. I will ask him to arrange your marriage in the same Nelamangala hall."

But he didn't receive the call. It kept ringing continuously. I too then asked my father to pick up the call, but he wouldn't. He'd turned to the other side, avoiding me. The phone continued to ring, and I jerked in the bed to find that it was my phone that was ringing.

It was Sandhya who was calling. I picked it up fumbling with the phone. "Hi Sandhya," I tried to get to terms whether I was still in the dream or had woken up. Why would Sandhya call me back?

"What does it mean when you say that I must have already moved on? You think getting into a relationship every few months is my hobby and I know how to move on quickly?"

"No Sandhya. I didn't mean in that way."

"And what was that pricking point you added? I must have already found someone? How sarcastic can you be!"

"I meant well for you...hoping you will find someone deserving of you."

"I cannot hear you properly. There is a connection issue," she said. It was already embarrassing listening to her rip me apart, over that, such technical connectivity issues were making me repeat myself, further putting me in a tight spot.

I did try to repeat it for her, but I don't think it was going through.

"What audacity you have, Raj? For eight whole months you don't even try to get in touch with me, and all of a sudden you call me to give some enlightened speech! You think I was waiting for you to show pity on me?"

"No Sandhya, all I did was accept my fault. Where does pity come into the picture? You are getting it all wrong."

"Of course, Mr Setty! You are always right. It is always others who misunderstand you, isn't it?"

"Sandhya please listen to me. I don't know why you have associated all the negative aspects for things I said to you. I really wish for you to be happy. I am saying that you are the one who was always right."

"I cannot hear you properly, Mr Raj."

"Wait, let me step out and speak." I opened the front door, to find someone standing right there. I panicked dropping my cell phone, and it became clear to me that it was Sandhya.

"Hi Sandhya, I didn't realise...Come in!"

"No, I will not come in," she bluntly said. It was impossible to read her expressions in the darkness.

"Please come in Sandhya. It must be quite late in the night. It won't be good if you stand outside."

She reluctantly came in, and I then switched on the lights in my room. Her eyes were tired and she had been crying, I could see. She looked very weak, which was not a matter of a few weeks. It must have been months. It was all because of me.

"You want some water?" I asked her.

She just shook her head, not even meeting my eyes.

"Sandhya, what am I to gain by trying to use sugary words? I have already lost you. I have only been trying to own up my fault in all these. Why do you feel it is wrong?"

"Of course these are sugary words of yours to escape clean from the relationship and not feel guilty about it."

"I will continue to feel guilty all my life, Sandhya."

"I cannot understand this. You had already ended everything eight months ago. Why did you have to rake things up? I was fine with the way I was."

"I didn't mean to open up old wounds, Sandhya."

"You have learnt to play with words like a typical team leader."

"No, I...sorry how do you know?"

"What?"

"That I have been promoted?"

She kept silent.

"Prakhar told you?"

"Yes, so?"

"Nothing."

"If you were going through hell all these months, why on earth couldn't you call me at least..." she said and tried to stop abruptly.

"I...I think...it was a necessary learning for me."

"So you learn your lessons and call me to keep me informed about that, and move on is it?"

"No Sandhya."

"Every other day I have been waiting for you to call me, but you don't! Finally I had to call up Prakhar and he tells me that you are trying to get some property. He'd called me last week to tell me what you were going through. I was getting desperate to call you, but he asked me to wait for your call. Today he updated me about your promotion, and I was waiting for your call. But you call me to tell me you want to wash your hands off me?"

"Why will I want to wash my hands off you, Sandhya?"

"Obviously because you have gotten over your infatuation over me, and now want to get married to some girl in your own community."

"Come on Sandhya, you know it was not infatuation between us."

"Then how come I see it's ended so well at your end?"

"I always have loved you Sandhya. Even in these months, each day, I thought about you, and I will continue to."

"All of it is rubbish. Had you loved me, you would not have been seeing me sit and cry in front of you. You would have embraced me long back and..." I pulled her to me and held her in my arms tightly, as she cried profusely. I had never seen her cry before, and I felt that I was the most disgusting person in the world to have been the reason for it.

We held each other for a long time, and she had now got her emotions in control. "I think I must be going now. It's late."

"It's late. So you are not going anywhere now," I told her.

"It's just one in the morning. I will manage."

"I am not letting you go now Sandhya."

"I don't like to stay in a stranger's house"

"And hence you will stay with me."

"Who are you to me?"

"If you think I can be given another chance, I will be the happiest person in the world."

"How can I trust you? You have broken my trust once."

"And through that, I have learnt the most important lesson in my life. So I request you to give me another chance."

"What is it that you learnt?" she said amidst sobs.

"That come what may, I will not let you go."

She rested in my arms for some more time. "Okay, it is getting too warm. Leave me."

I released her from my tight grip.

"See, right now you told me you won't let me go and within seconds you left me," she said.

I smiled and shook my head, while I held her beautiful face in my hands and pulled her to me again to embrace her. "I won't let you go Sandhya. I just cannot. Thank you for giving me another chance."

That just made me feel complete.

The next day, I called in sick, and so did Sandhya. It was not entirely a lie. The previous evening was an emotionally charged up one and we both were extremely drained. Also, there was just a lot of catching up to do for the past eight months. I took her through each instance that I had faced in the last few months, which made her both laugh and feel sorry at the same time.

"But then, what have you decided? Do you want to explore more options on plots?" she asked me.

"No, at least I am not sure for now. It has exhausted me both mentally and physically. We will work it out methodically, then explore to see what makes more sense."

"Hmm...After you broke up with me, I thought of involving myself in the apartment thingy. But then, in a couple of months, I lost interest as I was getting more hassled at a personal level." I continued to look at her, and she just shrugged.

"So let's do this. Let me get my remainder amount from Mr Nair. Once that is confirmed, we will sit and work out the options of an apartment or a land for the time being. Once we make a final decision..."

"No wait, time please" Sandhya interrupted. "What I did realise in those months when I spent time exploring apartment options was that even a simple and decent apartment would cost me a lot. So that option can be ruled out."

"No, but if we go for an apartment, then we will go together Sandhya. We have to then take a joint loan."

"Why will bank give joint loan to us? They don't have any boyfriend-girlfriend schemes yet."

"Eh...I know they don't have such schemes, Sandhya."

"Then?"

"They do have joint loans which husband and wife can take."

"What? You mean? We both...then..."

"What are you talking, Sandhya?"

"Well, I don't know. Are you hinting at something?"

"Yes, I have been telling you since last night that I cannot lead my life without you. What else could you interpret? Unless you thought I will marry someone else, and then continue having an affair with you all my life."

She threw some stationery items at me from the table. "You always have this thing of ruining a special moment Raj."

"Sorry," I went to her and held her close and she couldn't throw anything else at me.

"But Raj, would your father be okay?"

"Honestly speaking, I don't know. But we need to proceed with a lot of caution. I want him to accept us whole-heartedly, and not consider it as a compromise."

"I agree. I cannot live with guilt like that."

"Let's see how we should approach talking to him. I was thinking if I should ask Prakhar to intervene."

"Bad idea. Poor Prakhar cannot coordinate sitting in the U.S. Unless, you want to wait for him to come down."

"No, you are right. Prakhar might be close to me, but he is not necessarily as close to my dad."

"Do you think it helps if I talk to him? Or can I ask my father to talk to Uncle?" Sandhya asked.

"Wait! Your father knows about us?"

"No, he doesn't. Not yet. But considering even my parents' was an inter-community marriage, I don't think he will have that big an issue. Also, for some random reason, he likes you a lot."

"Wow! Your dad likes me, is it? That's great news."

"Okay now tell me if it helps if my father talks to yours?"

"I actually don't know, Sandhya. I think it will have to be me. I just need to think through how I speak to him."

Sandhya couldn't help feeling sad, "What if he says no? For all you know he hates me."

"No Sandhya. I've discovered a lot about my father lately."

"Eh...okay."

"It's as if in the past few months I've learnt a lot about my father," I told her with a lot of seriousness.

Sandhya smiled, and that almost turned into a giggle.

"What?"

Her giggle continued to become mild laughter.

"Come on. Here I am trying to talk on a serious topic, and you are laughing mindlessly."

"I just laugh on how naïve you are."

"How naïve I am? Meaning? I just said that I have learnt a lot about my father in the past few months."

"Or my beloved one, maybe you have learnt a lot about yourself in the past few months, and hence are able to appreciate how wonderful a person your father is."

She wasn't giggling anymore. At the moment, she looked so mature, and sounded so sorted. She was looking through me like a glass.

She had made, what I will always regard, one of the most insightful statements that I've ever heard about myself. I was dumbfounded. At the outset, I really wanted to give her a witty answer, but the beauty of her statement was that it took its time to sink in and left me a bit more settled, as her smile spread to me. "Okay fine, you win."

"As always," she said, trying to lift her shirt collar that didn't exist.

"Okay, so what I was trying to say was that I think my father is not that unreasonable a person. So there is hope."

"What if he out-rightly says no?" she sounded concerned.

I didn't have an answer, "I don't know. But let's take it one at a time."

"I know it's not right to go against your father's willingness."

"Sandhya, hold on to your thoughts. Let me talk to him."

"Let's agree on one thing, Raj."

"What's that?"

"If your father disagrees..."

"Please Sandhya, let's not get into that negative mode."

"No, this is the realistic mode. Listen to me please. In case you father is not happy with you and me getting together, then I think...I think we should call it off."

"Are you mad! What's with you Sandhya?"

"Raj, before we split some months ago, I honestly hadn't thought about all this. Our time away made me think about a lot of things. A lot of things that we perhaps had taken for granted. It is simple, I don't think I will be happy with you, if our union has no consent from your father. I know you don't want to admit at this point in time, but I am sure even you would not want us to go ahead without your father's consent."

This was a dull end to our day of getting together. Her eyes were moist, but she still smiled. The thought of losing her was frightening indeed. I pulled her to me to hold her in a tight embrace.

Sandhya insisted that I speak to my father as soon as possible. She said it is the Band-Aid approach. It seems certain things you just need to rip off without dragging.

It was the next day, and I'd gone directly to see my father from my office.

It's so easy when you sit alone and think that this is exactly how I would be approaching things, and it all adds up so well, making you think that you were actually worried about such trivial matters in life. It is all fine when you are riding the bike on the way to your father's place, ready to spill the beans about your lovely girlfriend, and a minor point about her being from a different religion. When you are nearly there, just parking, and one or the other small point comes to your mind, and you realize there is no going back. Fear comes running to you at a pace even Bolt will be proud of. You start to get worried and wonder how on earth you thought you will talk to your father about it, and you panic further. Then you get on to your bike again, with an intention to ride back at the topmost speed, but then you see that your father, who had gone to the nearest Nandini outlet and is returning with a packet of milk, calls out spotting you as you were about to start your bike to scoot.

He was very surprised with my visit, more so because I was emphasising that there was no actual reason for the visit. He decided to make coffee for both of us, giving me time to ponder over things.

"How come you came without calling? That too so early. I was about to go on for a long walk after coffee. What if I had gone away by the time you reached?"

"Yeah, I just managed to ensure I caught you, isn't it? Only if I were ten minutes late..." I thought out aloud.

"So? Did you hear about any plots or something that you came to update me about?"

I shook my head with disappointment. Obviously I showed way more than I actually felt, "Really Dad!"

"Really son?"

"You really think I need a reason to come and meet you?" I tried to look pained.

"Oh my god!"

"What?"

"Since when?" What! How the hell did he figure out?

"Dad....?" He looked disturbed.

"You cannot hide it from me, Raj."

I mean this was stunning deductive capability. Even the Sherlocks and Poirots and Jeeves of the world would have fallen way short of such method and approach and psychology of the individual.

"How did you figure it out, Dad?"

"It's written all over your face"

"Oh..."

"Have you taken any tablets?"

"Huh?"

"Coffee isn't recommended for stomach upsets, son. Please return your glass."

"Oh no Dad!"

"Come on now, I know I make good coffee. But no use making it difficult for yourself this way."

"No Dad! I am completely healthy."

"You are not trying to lie to your father, I hope. I could read through that painful expression on your face. That used be the same expression that you used while you had tummy upsets in your childhood."

"I am going to take an oath that I shall never use such expressions again."

"Okay okay."

I took some more time to compose myself, and then understood that the more time I took, the more difficult it would become. So I decided to part with the information immediately.

"So Dad, you had been talking about acquaintances for my marriage..." I spoke in an unusually loud tone; which is normal to me when I am very nervous.

"Oh! Wonderful! So can I go ahead and talk to Revathi's father?"

"Wait Dad, please!"

"Sorry, go ahead."

"Dad I have found someone." I had let it out.

"Oh, you mean you have selected some girl for your marriage? All by yourself?" he asked.

Now that didn't sound encouraging.

"Yes, Dad." I was extremely scared at the moment.

"That's bad, Son."

"But why Dad? I always thought it won't be an issue with you if I found someone."

"No, I am referring to the shaking of your leg while you are having coffee. That's bad manners."

"Oh, you mean... sorry."

"The table and half the room was shaking. Anyway, so you say you have someone who is the right girl?"

"Eh...yes Dad."

"So, go ahead and tell me more. Who is this girl? What does she do? Since when you have known her? Tell me more."

"Yes, Dad. It's...it is Sandhya." There you go. The truth was out.

"Wait Raj! You mean Sandhya Johnathan?" Dad had widened his eyes.

"Ahem...It is Johansson Dad. But yes, the same girl. You have known her for long."

He didn't touch his cup of coffee again for a long time, as he seemed deep in thought.

"What happened Dad? Please say something."

"Does her father know about this? What does he have to say?"

"Not yet Dad. She's yet to talk to him." I wanted to say more, but he turned aside thinking through something.

"I want to meet Sandhya."

"Oh...er...sure Dad. I will get her here tomorrow."

"No, now. I want to meet her today."

"Sure, Dad. I will go get her."

"No, ask her to come directly. It makes no sense for you to travel all the way back." He looked at a distance.

▲

"What? This was unforeseen. He wants me to come like now?"

"Yes, that's what he said."

"And he didn't want you to come and pick me? That does not sound encouraging, Raj." Sandhya's voice was very weak.

"I know, but let's see. Can you come now?"

"Of course. I am just nervous."

"Please don't be. You come down now. Let's see."

▲

Sandhya reached in less than a quarter of an hour to my utter surprise.

"He's inside."

"Should I have come in a sari or something?"

"No time for all that Sandhya. Just come, it's okay."

I took her to the living room where my father was waiting, keeping himself busy with a novel in his hand.

"Dad...this is Sandhya."

"I have met Sandhya before, Raj. Come Sandhya, please sit down."

"Hi Uncle," she nervously sat next to him.

"Hmmm...So Raj tells me something." My father looked at Sandhya, expecting her to speak.

"Yes, yes Uncle."

"Can I hear it from you, child?"

"So Uncle, I...we...kind of...thought it will be a good thing."

"Child, can you please be clear?"

"Yes Uncle, of course. I meant that both Raj and I like each other, and want to spend the rest of our lives together."

"Hmm.... I see."

Sandhya and I stole a quick glance at each other, not knowing where this was headed.

"But Sandhya, I see one big problem, and then there are several minor ones."

"Yes Uncle?"

"See, it is an obvious point that you and Raj are from different communities..."

"Yes, Uncle. I am aware."

"Right. The point I would like to bring in here is that I am not for once saying that one community is greater than the other. I think that is the most false statement and extremely drastic. Any person who believes in such statements, I can assure you, will never be my friend. But we all have to honour one universal truth, and that is, communities lead to difference in culture and upbringing. And these aspects would have gotten into your values and beliefs, some visible to you, but most of them deep rooted into your subconscious. On the outset, yes, many say that communities won't matter, but when you live with someone over a prolonged period of time, you slowly begin to observe these differences." My father paused and looked at the two of us.

The theory was indeed a profound one. I could see from the corner of my eyes that even Sandhya nodded her head.

My father continued, "Contrary to the same theory, I agree and accept that just because you get together with someone from the same community, does not mean you will have a wonderful relationship."

Both of us nodded.

"It simply means kids that if you have realistically, and not just emotionally, decided to marry each other, you will be tested throughout your lives on these small points. More than a few times, you will be tempted to take the easy way out. But that's when your will and your willingness to be with each other and for each other will count."

We nodded again.

"It is up to you to learn to forgive each other, correct each other and forget things that are to be forgotten when the time comes. If you think you have come here to convince me on your marriage, then that should be the least of your priorities. I just want you two to be convinced about things. Because kids, there will come a day when I won't be around to tell you whatever little I have learnt from life. It will then be up to you to keep up with each other the promises you have made."

I just gulped at what my father had said, and Sandhya looked at me.

"What is your father's opinion about this, Sandhya?"

"Sir, he is..."

"What? Why are you calling me, sir?" My father questioned Sandhya.

"Sorry, I mean Uncle..." She was clearly nervous. "What I mean is, I don't know if Raj has told you, but the thing is even my parents' was an intercommunity marriage. My father, many times in the past has explicitly mentioned that he would be completely comfortable with any culture. And in the last several months when Raj wasn't talking to me..." she paused, and bit her lips.

My father cast a fleeting glance at me, and returned to Sandhya, "Go on."

"Ahem...so when Raj and I weren't speaking for some months recently, my father wasn't happy that I was not in touch with Raj, and has given cues in a lot of instances that he likes Raj a lot."

"Hmm...Okay then," my father retired to his recliner. He seemed to be thinking about a solution to a certain problem.

"Yes Dad?" I asked, probing him.

"Now that I have spoken about all minor problems, before I come to the big one, do I understand I have your promise that it is fair for me to expect that you will adhere to what I just said?"

"What?" I could not contain myself. "You mean Dad, what we have been talking about till now are all minor problems according to you?"

"Yes, of course."

"Sir then...I mean, Uncle then, what is the big problem that you were talking about?"

"But I don't know whether you both agree to the minor points I just spoke about at length?" My father looked at us demandingly, and continued before one of us could open our mouths, "And I understand these are no checklists for you to put a tick mark against right now. But these are on-going things throughout your lives."

"Yes, Dad," I said.

"I agree Uncle. You've articulated it very well. But I went through these while I was not in talking terms with Raj for some months, and I am convinced that he will be the one I will be spending my life with," Sandhya said.

I held her hand, and said, "Me too" in not so loud a tone.

She smiled and continued, looking at my father now, "And Uncle, I don't mean to disrespect you, and I mean this in a very serious way. Many elements that you just pointed out about forgiving, forgetting and correcting, are the things that I have already started doing with Raj."

"Oye! That's not fair," I shouted.

But my father raised his hand and I fell quiet. Now I could understand that this raising hand business was something I had inherited from my father. His smile was now gone, as he cleaned his glasses and then looked up at Sandhya.

"See, all the problems we discussed till now are things that you both need to take care about. The one big problem is what I need to take care about."

"What is it Uncle?"

"Please don't take this in a wrong way. I mean no offence Sandhya," began my father as Sandhya took a big gulp.

"Dad, whatever it is, I am sure we will face it. Please trust me."

"Eh...this I don't know son."

"It's ok, Uncle. Let us know the big problem in your mind that's bothering you so much."

"Sandhya, I am sorry child. But it is very difficult for me to remember your father's name. I always call him Johnathon and Raj here corrects me and refers to some name that I usually forget. I am really worried how to ensure that your father does not take me wrong, you know?"

There was a minute of silence, he looked at us again and said, "What? It is not a joke."

"Dad!"

"Uncle? Are you serious?" Asked Sandhya, with a lot of excitement.

"What is it child?" My father asked Sandhya.

"It means you are okay for the marriage?" she asked, unable to hide her joy. Then it struck me that he had already implied his consent to our marriage.

"My consent, as I said already, is of no relevance. However, if you still want me to give my opinion. I refrain from judging people, but the truth is that at my age it is quite simple to look through people. All I can say is that you are a nice and at the same time very smart kid. I hope my son has realised, he is extremely fortunate to have you by his side."

I was totally flabbergasted to react, and I couldn't see Sandhya saying anything either. We were still digesting what we had heard.

"And why are you both silent? You two still want to marry each other, right?" asked my father.

I ran up to him and hugged him whilst he was on his chair, and Sandhya immediately joined us, her hand on his knees, as he invited her to the small family union wrapping his arms around both of us.

It was a couple of months after the day we'd got my father's consent. Mr Johansson, as Sandhya had assessed, was quite pleased with the news that he would have me as his son-in-law. While I am no modest guy, let me tell you that it was a pleasant surprise to me, for I didn't know what he'd seen in me to like me. Of course, it was a question that would not reach him ever.

It was a sunny Saturday, as four of us – Sandhya, her father, my father and I – were seated at the table just after lunch, and there was a debate taking place.

"Church marriage or temple marriage? I am okay with either," said Mr Johansson.

"I agree Mr Johansson, either is fine with me as well. However, I don't want it to be a costly affair."

My father had managed to remember my future father-in-law's name correctly.

"But sir, it is just one daughter I have."

"Yes sir, I understand that. But there is no use spending so much money on a wedding to please others." I, who had always thought of my father as stingy, and even now he was making a statement which on the surface would have felt like that of a stingy natured person, still saw his point.

"What do you both kids think?" asked Mr Johansson.

"I think Uncle is right Pops. We can have a church wedding and a temple wedding, but we need not spend too much money," said Sandhya.

"Instead sir, let the kids save that money and use for something for their future. Don't you think so?"

"Yeah Pops, we can use the money to invest in an apartment's down payment or something." Sandhya became conscious and looked at me, "I mean, apartment or any other investment, you know."

"Hmm...I see I am clearly outnumbered," said Mr Johansson, not very happy.

"Sir, please don't feel bad. I am not saying that we will carry out the wedding in poor light or keep it too low key. All I am requesting is that let's not splurge all the savings just for a day, while that can be used for something more constructive for these kids' future. Having said that, I am still okay if you all feel otherwise."

Before anyone says anything, Sandhya said, "Pops, I think Uncle is right."

"Okay okay, but as Mr Setty has said, we will keep a balance. I cannot keep it too low key as well," he said, and we had reached an agreement.

"And Raj, I think Sandhya is right about the apartment."

I just looked at him, while I could see Sandhya was focussing on me to read my expressions.

Sandhya spoke before I could, "No Uncle. We can think about good plots of land. I used apartment just as a reference for any investment."

"No Sandhya," I interrupted. "Dad and you are right. There are too just many options that Dad and I have weighed over the last months on plots of land. But the bitter truth is that we middle-class people have no chance of buying a plot of land in the city, nor it is any easy to buy at the outskirts. I think we should try and get a good apartment," I concluded.

Sandhya was not very joyous at this, and let her hand find mine, which I felt was comforting.

▲

Sandhya, I must say, had done a lot of homework on apartments while we had stopped speaking. Yes, I have stopped calling it a break-up as the other reference seems more suitable. While she could not go ahead and afford them, she'd still created a good database for us to fall back on.

Now that I had managed some savings for nearly a year, and then again shockingly so Mr Nair had returned our due amount, and then some of Sandhya's savings put together, we were sure we could explore venturing into apartments again.

Out of some good number of developers' properties that Sandhya had shortlisted, we managed to cover all of them in a matter of three weekends and shortlisted a few of them, and ranked them as well.

Sandhya suggested, even before I could, that we obviously ought to take my father through these before closing in on any of the apartments. We had got a pre-used car from a portion of the money that had come from Mr Nair. We took him around showing each one of the apartments, and proudly listed down the pros and cons of each of the visited properties in a very detailed manner. According to me and Sandhya, out of these, there were at least three potential opportunities to invest in.

It was a strange thing that my father, who used to have many comments on each of the plots that we visited just a few months ago, had little or almost nothing to say about these apartments that we showed. I gathered that his interest levels and also thereby the knowledge about apartments were limited.

We reached late in the evening, and it was indeed quite tiring as we were out all day.

"What do you think Dad?" I asked intently.

"I think, I need a cup of strong filter coffee," he said, and went in to make three cups of the beverage.

Sandhya and I waited patiently.

Once we took a few sips of coffee, he said, "Kids, the options you showed me; a couple of them are quite far from your offices. What was the reason for shortlisting them?"

It was a simple question, "For investment, Dad."

"How investment? You will still be paying rent for the house you stay in, right?"

"Right Dad, but a couple of things. One, we will get some tax exemption as it will be a home loan that we will be applying for, and secondly, while we will pay both rent on the one hand and EMIs on the other, from a long term standpoint, we still will end up owning this apartment, no?"

"See there is no one right answer is what I feel Raj. But it is my frank opinion. Never venture into an apartment if you are not going to stay in it. It is not a great investment opportunity, if you think about it."

I wanted to argue, but my father wasn't done yet. "You are aware that an apartment obviously has no land value. Thus, there is no appreciation of the value in any manner. There is only depreciation on the building. Isn't it, commerce student?" he directed the last bit to me.

"Well yeah but..."

"Secondly, the resale value of apartments isn't very great. If I recollect correctly, once an apartment has aged for twenty years, no banks will even entertain a home loan."

"What? Is it?"

"So it does not make sense that you keep paying back the loan for some fifteen years, staying in some rented place, while you are not even getting any good returns on this. Hence, it cannot be categorised as an investment; at least not a good investment. I do agree that if it is some good branded builder, then there may be a question on a certain kind of appreciation, but that's hardly anything."

My Dad pretty much had bulldozed our first plan on investment. Mr Johansson also joined us.

"I completely am with you on this Mr Setty. Kids, please don't think of apartments as an investment. Go for apartments only if you believe you want to reside there."

"Hmm..." Sandhya and I nodded at each other.

"Then on the other two or three that are relatively accessible from your office space, let's spend some time on those," he said, sounding like an auditor, who had destroyed a process documentation by making note of several loopholes and now moving to the next process.

He keenly looked at the paper cut-outs of each of those apartments and then looked at us, "Surely not bad choices, but none of these seem to be from a branded builder, and also the cons that you both have mentioned in these are surely worth making note of, isn't it? One of them is adjacent to a school, the other is relatively an old building and the other is very near to a slum. Even the approaching roads to a couple of these weren't great. Hope you had future prospects in mind while trying to shortlist these."

Yes, my father sounded quite critical, but Sandhya seemed to not mind that, though it was slightly pricking me.

"But Papa..." Sandhya began. She had begun to call my father 'Papa' very recently. "See the bigger brands that are anyway in the centre of the city or any place that is easily accessible are highly priced. Even if between me and Raj we would manage to get through the EMIs, the initial investment in terms of down-payment is not something that we will be able to afford. So we had to consider those aspects before we could make this list," she completed.

"Precisely the point I was coming to." My father nodded to himself.

"Didn't get it Dad," I said thinking he forgot to take us through what he meant.

"So I wanted to tell you both, and good that even Mr Johansson is here, that I have decided to sell the plot of land that's in my name and I am sure that will make a good sum for you to use for the initial down-payment."

Remaining three there, said a loud "No!" in unison.

"What? Why?"

"No way Dad! That's yours Dad, and there is no way I am using it for anything."

"Don't be stupid son. What's an asset that does not come to use when you need it?"

"No Papa, it's not okay. Let's move to some other option."

"I agree with the kids Mr Setty. I cannot speak detailed logic like you, but I for sure know that in troubled times, such assets do come to use."

"Correct, and hence I want to use it now."

"No, Dad."

"And Papa, wasn't it you who had once said to Raj that it is a very silly deal if we exchange land against an apartment?" said my fiancé. I will be honest that I didn't remember that instance, but if she's saying it, it must be so.

"That's a great point, my child. You are right. But I am weighing different options here. This plot I own, as you all know, is not in a great location as Raj always highlights. So I don't think it is of any use to me. My needs are more than met by my pension, and thanks to the government service that I was in, my health insurance and stuff are covered. So you see the logic, don't you?"

"Dad, please. I myself am guilty about being cheap in bringing this up many times that it is near a sewerage canal and all that. Having said that, over the past months, I have known that it is not a joke to own a plot. That is like your legacy Dad. How can we let you sell it off?"

"Okay now, let's not get unnecessarily sentimental, kids. Here's the plan. While we all are clear about the location of the land, the fact remains that it is in Bangalore. So I am sure it will be worth something good for sure. I mean, even gutters cost a lot in Bangalore I guess. So I have little doubt about it. I didn't offer this suggestion earlier during our quest Raj, because there was no meaning in selling one piece of land for another. However, now it's a matter of a residence."

"But..." I began, and the hand went up again, asking me to hold on till he completed.

"I am sure this will be a very good contribution to the down-payment, and thereon you both, I am sure, will take care of the EMIs. I had made a call to Mr Joshi yesterday. He is the chairman of the society where I own the land. He could not speak properly yesterday as he had stepped out, but I have told him that I would visit the plot on Sunday, which is tomorrow. I didn't want to bring up the point on selling and stuff during the telephone call. Those things are always better spoken face to face. Now Mr Johnathon, do you mind a cup of coffee?"

"Oh, that will be nice, thanks. Er...did you call me Johnathon?"

"No no, I said Johansson. Must be the strong evening winds," my father said, and went into the kitchen.

My father just wouldn't let any of us talk about the matter anytime during the rest of the day. I never knew my father could be this adamant, and had to add this fact to the list of things I've recently discovered about my father.

Neither Sandhya nor I had the last many weekends to ourselves, as we were busy trying to zero in on the apartment. Even this weekend was going to be the same. While my father wanted to go alone and meet Mr Joshi, I decided to join him. Since Sandhya wanted to accompany us, I took the car out.

Mr Joshi, we saw, was a very diligent and respectful kind of a person, which was a pleasant surprise, for my opinion about such society chairmen isn't that great. He met us much before the entrance of the society at the said time without any delay.

He hugged my father as soon as he met him, which I felt was quite odd as my father is not a very physical person in that sense of things. "So when are you coming to stay with us in the society sir?" he asked my father, who very nicely dodged the question by introducing me and Sandhya.

"Oh! He is your son? How nice to meet you Raj."

He seemed to me to be someone easily excitable by the look of things.

"One small tiffin in our Darshini hotel before we go sit in our society meeting hall. In the hurry to meet you, I missed my breakfast. I hope that's okay," he offered.

I was quick to decline, and Sandhya tried to follow suit.

"Nothing doing. You have come here for the first time, and sir has come after more than two years. You are our guests. Please come now." He was not in a frame of mind to let us go un-darshinied, so we obliged.

Sandhya had something just to keep this chairperson's heart. I should have been intelligent to follow what she did, but before I did that, Mr Joshi had ordered a masala dosa each for him and me, which took time to arrive.

Sandhya and my father decided to walk towards the society, asking me to come in the car along with Mr Joshi once we were done. I understood that maybe my father wanted to look at his plot of land for one last time before we could discuss about putting the piece of land up for sale.

While at the hotel, I saw Sandhya and my father walking away from us at a distance, when Mr Joshi interrupted me, "Such a nice man your father, Raj."

"Yes, that's true," I acknowledged, and our breakfast arrived and we got busy eating.

The silence between us was getting awkward so I said, "You are a bubbly kind of person."

He shook his head vigorously, though the piece of dosa was still dangling outside his mouth, making me wonder the reason I had opened my mouth to ask such a question at such an important juncture.

Only after some good half a minute of his vigorous shaking of the head did Mr. Joshi speak, "Not true, not true," he said a bit loud for my liking.

I looked around to see if people were misinterpreting me in any manner, thinking I was accusing the local guy of some criminal activity. Thankfully, none was looking at us.

"Oh okay," I thought I should just end the conversation.

"What I mean is Raj…In my office, people say 'what Joshi, you don't smile often' or they say 'why so serious in life Joshi?' I am cheerful only with some people whom I really like."

"Oh, that's nice. So it makes my dad one of those few people," I offered.

"Yes, absolutely. No doubt. Sir is right there," he exclaimed.

"But what's the reason for that?"

"Why? Your father has not mentioned my story to you? Thanks to him. I got a beautiful piece of land in this Vaishakh society."

"How is that Mr Joshi?"

"See, I was new to Bangalore, and it took me only few years to realise that I wanted to settle in this city. I was looking for a good plot of land, so that I could construct a house in future. I got it in this society. Thanks to him."

"Oh, okay! Like that? So he referred you to this place?"

"No Raj. Most of the plots were already sold. He resold the land to me," Mr Joshi said. That kind of sent a shiver down my spine. I wanted to react immediately, but was worried that if I got excited, then there was a clear chance that Mr Joshi won't even continue talking. So I sat still.

"Okay that's nice. But he still has a plot of land there, doesn't he?"

"Er...you are so innocent Raj. I think it's with this generation. Even my teenage son is always in his own world and never listens to me. Of course he still has a plot of land. Because he exchanged his beautifully located plot with a lesser priced one."

"Hmm...." I said, but my heart was pounding like hell. What was he saying?

"So your father was one of the initial buyers and hence had opted for a plot located at the centre of this beautiful society. Unfortunately back then, one small portion of our society was adjacent to this Vrishabhavathi canal where Bangalore's filth flows. So plots in that portion were obviously difficult to sell. When I had approached the developers back then, I mean before the formation of our society, they told me that some person was in need of money and hence is looking to resell his plot. It turned out to be your father."

I gulped, and could say nothing.

"If I remember correctly, it was for some school thing of yours. I don't know too many details."

It dawned upon me that I was in a small-time school in my primary schooling days, and was moved to a reasonably good one as I entered my high school. Now if I thought about it, I knew it would have cost a lot, both in terms of donations and the fee expenditure.

"It is difficult for an honest government employee to match with the likes of these costly schools. Yes, I remember now, it was during the time of admission that I had approached him, and he didn't delay even a bit. He sold the plot to me, and bought the low priced plot near that canal. And moreover..." he had faded away, and I left him without excusing myself, too many thoughts in my head.

I went to the wash basin, as tears welled up and I cried. I never remember tears flowing down my cheeks this way before, as my throat pained and it was difficult to breathe. I cried for it wasn't actually the sacrifice, but it was the silence surrounding it that belittled me. I cried for it made me realise how small a person I was. I cried for I didn't think I had it in me to become a good person that I know my father is.

I tried to compose myself and washed my face to return to Mr Joshi.

"Hey, your eyes are so red. All okay?"

I cleared my throat, "I touched my eyes from the hand I ate the dosa, so..."

"You kids are not used to eating with hands, and are used to eating with forks and spoons I think."

He laughed at what he was saying, and I tried to join in. We kind of rushed after paying the bill to catch up with my father and Sandhya. I had determined that I would not let my father sell the plot, and would somehow convince him otherwise.

It was a beautiful society, and I could see there were hardly any plots that were empty. Houses had already occupied the place, and when we passed through a lane, Mr Joshi showed me his house.

I clinched my fist as my heart wrenched looking at the plot where his house was built. It was an excellent one and my father had given this away to choose the one near that infamous canal, only for my better future.

We saw that my father and Sandhya were waiting near Mr Joshi's house.

"Come come Joshi, I was just telling Sandhya that this is where you live. And Joshi, so many houses have come up. Last time I saw there were hardly any houses, and now there is not even a single empty plot that can be seen. It took a lot of time to locate your plot. I just happened to remember the number of your plot and with some difficulty we came here," he said.

"Of course sir, you will remember this plot number..." Mr Joshi wanted to continue.

"Yes, yes, but tell me how come so many houses have come up?"

"Yes sir. So the good part is that the adjacent big colony..."

"You mean the bank colony which had acquired many acres?"

"Correct sir. They have also developed their society beautifully, and after my discussion with their chairman for nearly a year, they have opened up the connecting roads between both our societies."

"That's very nice. I'm sure the people chose you rightly as the chairman."

"Thank you, sir."

"So both societies' roads are interlinked then. Hmm...But even then, how does that help in such a big way? "

"Sir, once you go through the bank colony, it will then connect to the ring road within a kilometre."

"Wow! That's wonderful. It had completely missed my thinking. Yes correct, so our society's back entrance will take you to bank colony and from there in some distance you connect to the ring road. Hmm...So the plot value also must be good now."

"Well yes sir, but why do you ask?"

"I am just checking. So there still is considerable difference between the plots here near your house and where my plot exists."

"Of course sir. It's difficult to even imagine buying plots in the lane that you have yours."

My father could not hide his disappointment.

"Why sir? Don't tell me you plan to sell it."

"No, we won't," I interrupted.

My father just smiled and shook his head. "Okay, anyway. Let's see it once before we can talk about it in your office, Joshi."

"Sir, tell me correctly. Are you planning to sell it?"

"Yes Joshi."

"Sir but why? I thought you will construct..."

"No we are not selling it." I was very determined.

My father took me and Sandhya aside, "What is it now Raj? I have already told you my decision. I want this plot to be useful in whichever way for you both to stay in your own house. I get it that Joshi is telling us that people might not buy the plot, but I am sure there will be some people who are desperate to buy. "

"Dad, come what may, I will not let you sell this plot. No matter what, and I am very very serious."

"Sandhya, please take him away from Joshi and talk some sense into him. I don't want Joshi to sense that we are not aligned."

"But Papa..." Sandhya herself wasn't very convinced, but my father left us to go to Joshi, and they continued to walk away.

Meanwhile, I told Sandhya what Mr Joshi had just told me in the hotel. She was overwhelmed with what she heard. "We cannot be so cruel to let Papa sell this plot, Raj."

"Exactly what I am saying Sandhya. We will convince him together. We will do that once we reach home."

"In fact, let's play along on selling. Else he will lose his cool." She agreed to my point.

We then went tracking my father.

"Phew, this is a big layout, man," said Sandhya, a bit tired.

"Yeah, Dad was saying back then it had some four hundred plots, making it one of the biggest layouts. Imagine we are not yet getting the foul stench of Vrishabhavathi. So we still need to walk a long distance I guess." I looked around to see that my father and Mr. Joshi were already returning, laughing at something.

"So Papa, what is the next step to sell the plot?" she asked bluntly. Poor Sandhya is a very straightforward girl. If you ask her to do something nice and good, she will come out scoring aces. However, to play a cunning hand and conspire others to believe in a lie, she will fail miserably. No wonder they say that the opposites attract.

I held her hand, and looked at Mr Joshi, "We can talk about the details in the confinement of your society office Mr Joshi." I looked straight into his eyes, as crooked and rogue-like as I could. Well it comes naturally to me, so it wasn't that difficult.

"I have decided not to sell the plot," said my father.

I mean, come on guys. We need some consistencies in life. "Dad, even politicians hold on to their views for longer time than you did."

"Ha ha!"

"Of course I am happy that you have decided not to sell, but..." I shrugged as my father slapped my arm laughingly. I think it's all this Vrishabhavathi's fault. The foul stench in it has some chemical that may make people go bonkers.

Sandhya and I, ignoring the elders, walked towards the said plot, trying to track the number, as the elders followed us again.

Sandhya saw a park and we thought we would walk through that pleasant path adjacent to the park. There were houses, or should I say huge villas that were built and the make of the cars outside indicated that there resided a very posh set of people. The roads were very wide. Even though it was not early in the morning anymore, there were so many birds chirping away.

"How far do you think Papa's plot is?"

I didn't answer, as I stared at the deep end of the road. It was a dead end. I turned around now to see that if I leave out the entrance we took, there was only one other exit, and that would take us to the bank colony.

Something gripped me from within, and I held Sandhya's hand in mine and pressed. We were standing in front of the only empty plot in the whole lane, and the plot number matched with that of what my father's was supposed to be.

"Dad..." I pointed at the plot and then to him, as Sandhya followed my gaze very carefully.

"Ah yes, this is the plot," said my father standing close by.

I had no words to speak, and had goose-bumps on my hands, as I looked at the most beautiful piece of plot that I'd seen in all these months and I said, "Wottaplot!"

Even Sandhya was too shocked to speak, "How Papa?" is all she could manage. But my father, was just beaming his best smile and didn't say anything. It took time for us to absorb the whole thing.

"You knew?" I asked my father.

"No," he said.

"Where is that Vrishabhavathi?" I asked, still lost.

"Raj, I was telling your father just now that the civic amenities folks had covered the rubbish and have built a park over it. It seems they had received a mandate to not let the canal run through a residential area. It was actually closed nearly a couple of years ago. Remember Setty sir, I had asked all members to contribute a one-time amount for civic amenities purpose back then stating there are jobs to be completed in our society? This is one of them. Of course, we didn't have to bear all the cost. It was more of a government mandate. I am surprised how you missed it. It was a mail that was sent to your current residence."

"Yes, I vaguely remember, but I didn't know this…" my father's voice trailed off.

"Then Mr Joshi, why did you say a while ago that it's difficult for us to imagine people buying any plot in this lane?" I asked.

Mr Joshi, was equally confused as I was. "I don't understand why you ask that Raj. Look at it for yourself. A fine park opposite these plots, then a big road, nearness to the rear entrance of the society, which means people here will have the easiest access to the ring road and thus access to the main Bangalore city. Don't you think the cost will be too high for people to afford? So I said that it is difficult to imagine people wanting to buy it," he said, as the rest of us were still looking back at the plot every few seconds.

Mr Joshi got a call and excused himself for a moment.

"So after all, I think there is no need for you to look for an apartment. You can construct a house in this plot," said my father.

I hugged him from behind, and we continued to look at his plot in awe and Sandhya joined us.

"Not a bad decision after all that I bought this," said my father.

No, I couldn't afford to break into tears two times in the same morning. I have a reputation to keep folks. I held him even tighter, and Sandhya too tightened her grip on my hand. The tranquillity was not just seen in front of us, but I'm sure all three of us felt it from within. I closed my eyes and let the peaceful silence take over. It would be an insult to try and capture the feeling in words, and I wouldn't dare to either.

▲

How true it is that you aspire for something badly and work towards it with all you have and wonder why it keeps moving away from you. Only later you realise that something even better and incomparable is awaiting you in its place. I thought those were just stories and sayings to make people feel optimistic. I was here, experiencing that bliss though I hadn't imagined it in the wildest of my dreams.

A thought came to me as I was surrounded by the people whom I love – my father, my love and my friend Prakhar in my thoughts whom I hoped to meet in the coming weeks.

They say that you are nothing but the sum of choices you make in your life. I know I still have a long list of choices to make in mine. But they who said these words missed stating that it is not just a set of choices you make; sometimes you need to be fortunate that someone else makes the choice of being your best friend, someone else makes the choice of sharing their life and love with you, and someone who makes a choice to be an unconditionally loving parent. I might have gone wrong in some of the choices I made till now and I shall be careful in the future, but I shall be ever thankful that the others who mattered to me made the choice to make me a part of their world.